I0453796

THE
COMMITTED

ALSO BY Justin Mermelstein

Glimpse
A Week and Some Change
Nowhere in Particular
The Spirit of Magic
A Time to Commune

THE
COMMITTED

JUSTIN MERMELSTEIN

LuBelle
Publishing

Copyright © 2015
The Committed | Justin Mermelstein
All rights reserved.

This book is licensed for your personal enjoyment only.
If you've stumbled across this book without
purchasing it and you like what you've read,
please support the arts and purchase a copy.

Any resemblance to anything real is purely coincidental.

ISBN-13: 978-0-9886687-4-4

www.JustinMermelstein.com

For *the good parents, of whom I know many*

"It is easier to build strong children than to repair broken men."

—*Frederick Douglass*

"We're killing strangers so we don't kill the ones that we love."

—*Marilyn Manson*

PREFACE

Saturday, November 8, 2014, 7:22 PM

Arthur Parish wiped away the blood, ink, and plasma. The abrasiveness of the paper towel irritated the already raw patch of skin stretched over Codi Garret's ribs. She started at the sensation.

"I was lost before having my daughter," she said. "When you're young, you think you know everything. Not me. I didn't have a clue, and I had no qualms about it. I found a part of myself when Cara was born. And now that part is gone again."

Arthur glanced up from the half-finished tattoo. That's when he first noticed her eyes, so blue they were almost silver. "How long has she been gone?"

"Three months." She clasped a paper towel, wiping her face whenever the tears tickled her cheeks. "Fuck," she muttered under her breath.

"I know this hurts like hell. You're being a real sport."

She tried to force a smile, but the pain contorted it.

"Codi. Is that your full name?" he asked, attempting to distract her.

"Mmhmm." She hissed at the machine as Arthur lowered the needles again. They punctured the dermis, leaving behind a trail of blue ink. It pooled, concealing the path underneath until he wiped it using the towel moistened with surgical soap. She lay flat on her side and held the rolled bottom half of her thermal shirt in her right fist, her midriff bare up to her bustline. Her left arm, bent at the elbow, propped up her head. The chair, reclined nearly flat, was comfortable enough, though a bed of spikes might not have stolen her attention from the searing pain in her side. "My parents liked the name Cody when they thought I had an extra part." She wiped her eyes again. "Then they saw my vagina, changed a letter, and called it a day."

Arthur blurted out a laugh. "I like it."

"I never minded it. And when I named Cara, I figured I'd give her something similar. Not the same, but short and sweet, so maybe she wouldn't hate her name too much either."

Arthur rubbed a thin layer of ointment over the tattoo using the side of his pinky finger. "I feel like most people hate their name at one point or another, growing up. It's either too common or, in my case, not common enough. In junior high, I wanted to change my name to Kevin. Or Brad. I think it was

Brad." He shrugged. "I figured the chicks would dig me with a name like that. Arthur ... Art. It's an old man's name. Who wants to slow dance to Edwin McCain with an Arthur?"

She chuckled, trying not to move.

"But I hear you about short and sweet. We named our daughter May. Simple enough. She might get some shit about being named after a month, but maybe that'll be the worst of it. Hopefully."

Codi's breathing relaxed some, becoming rhythmic. "How old is your daughter?"

Arthur's foot slipped from the pedal. *Goddammit.* Why had he brought up his daughter? Codi didn't seem to notice the momentary pause. "She's three weeks old." He resumed tattooing. "I'm sorry."

Staring at the ceiling, she smiled. "If I expected the entire world to stop spinning just for me, I would've crumbled a long time ago. Other children still exist."

The front door opened and a flood of sound rushed in from the busy street outside. Arthur glanced up at the men, one holding the door for the other. Both were dressed in UPS uniforms, and both held cups of coffee.

"Hey, guys. Just appointments for today. We do walk-ins on Fridays and Saturdays. If you want to make an appointment, just let me know." They nodded and flipped through the flash art on the walls.

"I bet she's beautiful," Codi said, snapping Arthur's attention down to the table. After a moment of hesitation, he pulled off one of his black surgical gloves and fished in his back pocket for his phone. A picture of May when she was a newborn appeared on the home screen, and he turned it to Codi.

"She's precious," Codi said, her neck crooked back to see. "You're a lucky man."

"I know that even more now." He pocketed the phone and snatched a new glove from the box on the table to his right. The two men left the store.

"People are afraid to ask me about it. About Cara."

Arthur sure as hell was. But she'd exposed the elephant in the room. He pressed his foot on the pedal and went back to work.

"I mean, I get it," she said. "What the hell is anyone supposed to say to the girl who's had her daughter kidnapped? There's no small talk for that, is there?" She closed her eyes, removing herself from one pain and immersing herself in another. "But it makes you feel ostracized. I already know that I'm alone in this, but then I feel really, really alone."

The tattoo studio was one big room on West Mechanic Street, in the downtown district of New Hope, Pennsylvania. Black and white vinyl tile made up the floors, and the walls were painted white. The small section at the front of the store, where customers could lounge, serve themselves coffee, and watch TV, was separated from the artist's area by a long, cherry-stained front desk. There was no shop manager; the artists ran the entire shebang. To the right of the desk was a path to two stations manned by Alejandro and Mason. To the left were Arthur and Nayeli. Each station contained a tool chest for all equipment, a separate small table (where the jars of ink caps, cotton swabs, disposable razors, ointment packets, spray bottles, and other medical accouterments lived), a portable table on casters to keep handy any tattoo supplies currently in use, and finally the respective chairs of both the artist and the client. Each artist's station was the home of certain lucky charms, family pictures and other personal touches, but only Nayeli and Mason's areas included part of the back wall. Given that the entire room was visible, Arthur made sure to run a clean shop.

"What about your ..." Arthur began. "Is there a ..."

"No."

He swallowed.

"Cara doesn't have a father."

He felt guilty for asking the question. It was loaded for his own sake. He was madly attracted to her. And as a happily married man, it wrung his insides.

He wiped more ink from the red and swelling skin and shifted back a few inches to get a better look at his work. Satisfied, he lowered the machine to her flesh again. This time, Codi barely reacted. "Grandparents?"

"I live with my mom and dad, but half the time they're in a worse place than I am, so I have a select few friends I lean on, when they're around. They have their own lives. Most are married. Most have their own children."

A chill rippled along Arthur's shoulders, the reality of the woman on his table setting in. Tears welled in his eyes, and then one made the great escape, trickling down his cheek. He fought hard to restrain the rest, sniffling here and there, but Codi knew. The beginning of a cry, the middle, the end, she knew all phases and knew them well. Crying was a state of constant being.

The room, empty aside from the two of them, echoed at each word. "My mother put her in bed." Codi shifted her head on her folded arm. "Seven-thirty. Just like any other night. Cara changed into her pajamas, hid in her pile of stuffies until Grandma pretended she couldn't find her, sang *Star Light, Star Bright* three times, and went out like a light while her ..." her voice broke. She took a deep breath. "... while my mother rubbed her back.

"At about nine-thirty, it sounded like all the furniture in her bedroom lifted off the floor and crashed back down. Just this gigantic bang overhead. I sprinted up the steps and through her door and she was gone."

Arthur moved his eyes from her ribs to her face.

"The cops were there two or three minutes after I called. And three months later, we know nothing more than we did that night."

Arthur thought of his daughter, so brand new to

the world that her skin was still pink, her smell sweet. Thank goodness it wasn't him, he caught himself thinking. He tried to shake the feeling but the weight of Codi's situation wouldn't let him. And the likelihood of the conclusion. It made him sick. He wondered if Codi thought about it, too. Of course she did. Her nightmare was a walking, talking reality. There hadn't been anything she did *not* think about, of this he was sure. What a horrendous thing.

He finished her tattoo, working in near silence. When she reached into her purse for her credit card, he declined, holding up his hand. "There isn't a goddamned thing I can do but this. Please take it."

After some back and forth, she relented.

"I wish I could take all your pain away from you," he said. She hugged him and left the shop, waving through the window as she walked to her car.

Sunday, April 5, 2015, 9:18 PM

"Call the police!" Arthur shouted from the basement. He hauled himself up the shaky wooden steps and through the downstairs hallway, into the living room, where he came to a halt, listening for cries. Silence. He ripped back into the kitchen and threw open each cabinet door. They clapped into each other like off-kilter applause.

He'd been through each room twice, and his eyes were wet. Sweat loosened his slicked-back hair, tracing his forehead and dripping down the sides of his face.

"Arthur, she's not up here!" Sarah yelled from upstairs.

"Call the *fucking* police!" He'd never yelled at her in all their time together, it wasn't in his character. But his phone was charging on their nightstand upstairs, and, besides, why hadn't she called the police yet? He'd said it three times. That's when he noticed her phone on the island in the kitchen. He picked it up and fumbled around until he swiped to the password screen.

"What's your passcode?" he shouted as he stumbled up the steps.

"0-4-2-0," she said, hugging herself at the top of the stairs, her face beat red, body quivering.

His fingers trembled, and he entered the code incorrectly twice. He steadied himself. "My daughter is gone," he stammered into the phone. He felt ridiculous saying the words. They did not feel real. They could not *be* real. The 9-1-1 recordings on the news were just TV. Kids were never *actually* kidnapped. Horrible things like this did not exist in real life. "She was in her bedroom sleeping and now she's not. She's not in there. She's just gone." His voice became delirious. "Please send someone right now." He paused a moment, the operator responding. "92 Old York Road, white house, all the lights are on. Yes, I'll stay on the line with you." The operator asked Arthur for everyone to remain calm. Easy for her to say. She explained the police would be there very shortly. He only heard her instructions vaguely, enough to acknowledge them, but not enough to oblige. Periodically he would call out, expecting the baby to respond. She was six months old. But people do funny things when they're in a panic. In vain, he continued rushing around the house.

Sarah stood in place, still holding herself. When the first squad car finally arrived, sirens blaring, Arthur had the door open before the officers had even stepped out of their vehicles. He spoke frantically while meeting them halfway up the walk. "Please help us. Please find her." His legs wobbled and he squatted near the doorway, crying hysterically as he slumped. A second officer helped him to his feet, and he recognized the man immediately – Simon Shelley, a regular at The Paunched Pig, a bar Arthur frequented after work. He tried to escort Arthur to the living room, but Arthur refused. "I'll bring you to her room."

They followed him to the door but did not allow him inside. He tried to push through, but the first officer, his nametag read *Cannon*, took Arthur by his shoulders and requested cordially, without a trace of hostility in his voice, "Sir, it's best if you return downstairs now." He knew it was a sugarcoated demand. Sarah protested from the top of the stairs, but Cannon continued, even-keeled. "I'll have Officer Shelley here take the both of you down. He'll ask you some questions so that we can get this figured out as soon as possible, okay? That's the best way you'll be able to help us." Arthur nodded. He turned and took his wife by the hand, leading her down, ahead of Officer Shelley. Additional sirens squealed outside as seemingly the entire New Hope Police Department was called in.

Arthur and Sarah sat on the couch and watched as the flurry of cops blocked off the road and set up shop in and around the house. Shelley recognized the fear in both of their eyes as he sat at the edge of the loveseat to the right. He was big – 6'2" or 6'3", at least. He removed his hat and rested it on the edge of the glass coffee table, displaying a head as bald as a cue ball.

"They'll canvas this entire area, Arthur," said Shelley. "By foot, along the roads, everywhere."

A handful of officers entered the front door just as Officer Cannon came down the steps to meet them. One man, who Arthur assumed was the sergeant, barked orders. "Cannon," he said, "I need you and Cruz to search every inch of this place. Every nook and cranny. This child is six months old. She's not hiding or playing a game. Wherever she might be, she couldn't have moved around much." Cruz and Cannon began their hunt.

Sarah held her head in her hands.

"We'll have a team of detectives here who'll take over," said Shelley. "But I need to ask you guys a few questions if you feel like you can answer them."

Arthur stared into the foyer where the police were

congregating.

"Wilson," said the sergeant.

"Yes, sir," said an officer, stepping front-and-center.

"Get on the horn with SEPTA, Trans-bridge, Greyhound, Amtrak. If it moves out of this area, make sure they're aware."

"Yes, sir," he repeated, hightailing it out of the house.

"I need someone to notify the state police."

"On it," said another officer.

"Make all of Bucks aware too. The entire jurisdiction. Shelley is getting the info now and we'll put out the Amber."

"Arthur?" Shelley asked.

"Yeah. Yeah, go ahead and ask," Arthur said.

Shelley was obviously perturbed. New Hope, Penn11ylvania was not known for its child abductions, or much else in the way of hard crime, for that matter. He flipped open his notebook and clicked his pen alive.

"What was your daughter ..."

"May."

"May. What was May wearing?"

"A black onesie." He looked at Sarah.

"She had white socks on, too," Sarah said from behind her hands. She dropped them to her lap. "Her legs were bare."

"Does she have any hair yet?"

"A mop of it," Arthur said. "Brown. She's my

skin color – pale."

"When was the last time you saw her?"

"When we put her to bed."

"Who put her to bed?"

"I did." Arthur rested his hand on Sarah's thigh. She sat back against the cushion. "I read her a story. My wife watched through the monitor." He gestured to a screen next to them, on the corner table between the couch and the loveseat. "Just like every other night. Sang *Sweet Child O' Mine* until she fell asleep, shut off the light, closed the door, and came back downstairs."

"Then what happened?" Shelley asked, jotting down the story in shorthand. He turned to the next page and looked up.

"About, I guess, two hours later," Arthur answered without blinking, staring straight ahead, "we were watching TV and my battery died." He held up his phone. "I brought it up and plugged it in next to my bed. Put it on my nightstand. We only have two chargers. Fucking things are expensive."

Shelley chuffed some air from his nose.

"I turned to leave the room, was going to check on the baby, when it felt like the entire house moved." He turned to face Sarah again. "Like it went over a speed bump, it lurched, I don't know." He laughed without humor and dropped his head onto the back of the couch, then turned it to the Shelley. "We heard a loud cry. Like a whooping sound. I ran in and she was gone. Nothing was bothered. The window was closed and locked like it always is, and the door was closed when I rushed in. I'm sure of it. I remember not turning the knob enough and jamming my wrist. It was shut completely. And I never heard it open or close. I was right in the next room. I would've heard it. We didn't see or hear anything while we were sitting down here, either."

"Nothing on the video monitor?"

"No."

"This thing picks up everything," Sarah chimed in, her face now emotionless. "Any little noise."

Shelley nodded, noting it on his pad. "Did you enter the room?"

"I did," said Arthur. "I searched the closet, the corners of the room, anywhere I could think. I was only in there a few seconds, and then I ran out and checked the other rooms. Multiple times. Sarah came up, asked me what was the matter. I didn't want to freak her out, so I just told her to stay where she was and ran downstairs. I searched the entire house. The garage. The basement. Outside. Front and back. Everywhere. Twice. Then we called." He was starting to shiver, and the tips of his fingers were white from clenching his fists. He felt feverish.

"That's all I need right now," Shelley said. "The detectives will take over once they get here, and we'll get the Amber Alert out ASAP."

Arthur sat up straight and placed both hands on the couch next to him, ready to push himself to his feet. "You guys aren't leaving, are you?"

"No, we aren't going anywhere." He folded the pad and placed it in his shirt pocket, followed by the pen. "We're right here with you."

1.

Monday, September 28, 2015, 3:07 PM

Arthur struck the match and led it to the cigarette hanging from the corner of his mouth. The tobacco and countless other chemicals ignited with a bright and warm orange glow. He inhaled and closed his eyes, absorbing the nicotine and reveling in the momentary relief. He blew smoke from his mouth and nostrils while walking away from The Paunched Pig. "We've got nothing on him!" he screeched in the middle of the sidewalk. A tiny excuse for a dog yapped at him from a few feet away. Its owner pulled the white fluffy stuffed animal along as Arthur laughed at it, the cigarette still hanging from his mouth. "Not a fucking thing," he mumbled under his breath. "You hear that Sarah, they've got nothing on me, ya miserable fucking cunt!"

A gray-haired man seated on the outside patio of a restaurant with the rest his family looked up. "Sir!

Could you please watch your mouth!"

"Fuck you," Arthur said without looking back, stumbling along the display window next to him. He stretched out a hand to steady himself.

He'd been drinking. That day, and the many preceding. No one, friends or family, wanted to tell a man who had lost his only child not even six months ago to stop numbing himself. It was hard to consider him an alcoholic. In fact, he was bad at drinking. He had to force himself to binge, and, as he hated the taste of hard liquor, he was relegated to wine or beer, neither of which he was necessarily fond of either. But he was fond of being numb, especially after all of the formalities. The questioning. The accusations.

A child had gone missing under his roof. There were no fingerprints, no signs of breaking and entering or foul play anywhere.

He hadn't been charged. Oh, how they'd wanted to find a way to charge him, not because they didn't like Arthur, no, Arthur answered every question, showed up every time they'd asked him to come in. But *no one* ups and vanishes. The only logical conclusion was that Arthur, and perhaps even Sarah, was guilty. Guilty of at least … something. But their alibies were too strong. And too *true*.

The stigma wrapped them in a cocoon. Neighbors avoided them, ducking into cars or houses. Close friends and even some family stopped communicating with them altogether. The excuse was to give them their space, but the reality was unsent invitations and removal from social media.

At first, everyone *knew* Arthur and Sarah would never hurt their daughter, but by the second and third month, some doubt had begun to creep in. He *was* home. He didn't hear *anything?* Yeah, sure, it was still unlikely they were guilty of anything more than being negligent, but they still allowed it to happen, didn't they? By the fifth month, people starting calling for their heads.

Arthur banged into another storefront as he stumbled along Main Street. A large majority of the buildings were well over a hundred years old, some restored, some with a single coat of paint slapped over the rotting and decaying wood.

He swayed out into the middle of the sidewalk and steadied his drunken gait. He pulled the cigarette from his lips and it tugged at his skin, stuck in place by dry saliva, and caught a glimpse of his reflection in a car window. He moved in closer to inspect the man looking back at him. A mess. Hopeless and putrefying, rotting from the inside. His skin was pale, stretched across bones now visible more than ever. His normally full face was gaunt and ashen, and his cheekbones sank deep into his skull. He had dropped twenty pounds since April. Food repulsed him. Sleep repulsed him. *Being* repulsed him.

"Arthur, whoa, wait up."

He spun around, and the movement lurched his stomach. He bent over and immediately ejected his lunch: a plate of onion rings and a six-pack.

Pete, the bartender (and Arthur's friend since the opening of The Pig six years previous), was hurrying after him. "Hey, you all right, man? You don't look good. Maybe you should come back inside."

Arthur wiped the corners of his mouth with the belly of his black t-shirt. A tattoo peeked out from just above the belt of his jeans. He held up his other hand. "I'm cool. I don't think the onion rings were good." He spat next to the puddle of half-digested food and suds.

"Rings were fine, bud. You need to either come back to the restaurant or go to your shop before you get picked up."

"Shop," Arthur slurred, pointing a thumb down the block. "What did you come after me for? I forget to tip you?"

"What?" Pete wrinkled his forehead. "Oh, you didn't sign your receipt. Wanted to see if I could catch you."

"You caught me." He jotted his name on the bottom. "Just get in?"

"Yeah. Fredo's gonna get some shit for serving you this much."

"No one will know," Arthur said, spitting again.

"I do."

Arthur grinned.

"What's the word? Anything new today? They said you nearly fell off your stool laughing and continued right on out the door."

Arthur pulled out his phone and put it on speaker.

He played back a voicemail.

"Arthur, it's Grant. They're dropping everything against you guys. It's over. It's time to focus on May. Call me when you get this."

Pete threw up his hands. "Son of a bitch, man! That's great!"

Arthur nodded slightly. He had not expected the news. He had, of course, hoped they would clear him, but prepared as best he could for the worst-case scenario: going to prison and leaving no one to lead the charge for May. Grant, his lawyer, had warned him that this was a possibility. A very real one.

"Does Sarah know?"

Arthur shrugged. "Who gives a fuck. She'll find out eventually." He dragged from his cigarette one last time before stubbing it on the top of a garbage can and throwing it into its open mouth.

She had abandoned him like an animal. She *just couldn't handle it anymore*. Him, more specifically. Had she been wrong? He stared at a computer screen day-in and day-out, reading anything even remotely pertaining to child abduction. He watched from May's window, in the pitch black, all night, half-expecting the darkness to disclose what it had seen. He'd stare tree-to-tree and up and down the sidewalk. The drunker he got, the more he talked to himself. It would start as a mumble, a word here and there, and it would end with him screaming at the invisible son-of-a-bitch who had robbed him of his life. "How'd you do it, you piece of shit? Did you jump? With my daughter in your arms? Where'd you take her, you goddamned scumbag?" He'd throw his bottle out onto the grass, sometimes missing and shattering it on the sidewalk below.

She'd had it. It was too much to deal with. Her state of mind was fragile, spider-webbed as it was. If she snapped, there might not be any coming back. So she moved in with her parents.

"Call her and tell her, Arthur," said Pete.

Arthur shook his head. "Grant will call her. He's probably already talked to her. That's his fucking job. I'm sure I'll be paying him shortly, too." His eyes filled with tears, as they often did throughout the day. "I have to go back to work now."

Pete nodded. "Go ahead. Take it easy. Call me if you need to."

When Arthur was far enough away, Pete took out his phone and dialed a number. "Nayeli, it's Pete. Yeah, he's on his way back. He's shitfaced again." He waited. "Uh huh. Figured I'd give you the heads up. I'm going to fry Fredo. Take care of him today. Try to get him home if one of you can."

Thursday, October 1, 2015, 9:22 PM

"Nothing today, Arthur."

"So where do we go from here?"

"We let our guys do their jobs. That's what they're here to do. It's why they get paid. I'm telling you everything I've got, as

always."

"I just need you to level with me, that's all."

"You'll hear from the detectives before I catch wind of anything, anyway. I've told you that."

"Yeah. Thanks." He dropped the phone onto the windowsill and stared at it. The call ended and automatically returned to the home screen. May stared back at him. Her searing green eyes pierced his, locking him in. Finally able to blink, he wiped both eyes dry and picked up the phone again, scrolling to Sarah's name and selecting it. It rang four times before going to voicemail.

She was ignoring his calls.

How could it be over so quickly?

"I don't keep enemies," she had said once. They were studying in the school library for their final exams, at the same table where they had met four years earlier. Now it was senior year, and Arthur had already proposed.

"Remember that when you're my wife and I forget to take out the garbage."

"You do that now," she said.

He tapped his pencil on an open textbook, one of many in the sprawl of literature on the table in front of them. He shrugged in agreement. "So we're complaining. Okay, well, I can't tell you how many times I have to flush those friggin' balls of tampon toilet paper."

"*Ew!*" she gasped, shoving him from across the table. "You never have to do that. I don't flush tampons, jackass. They clog the pipes."

"You're right, you don't flush them." He grinned, staring at her. He stared a lot. It was easy for him to get lost in her face. She'd yell at him to stop, blushing even redder than her normal rosy complexion, but he couldn't help it. Her brown hair fell straight, way beyond her shoulders and down to the center of her back. Naturally straight, no equipment necessary. Her eyelashes were so long that they would entwine, making her blink them apart. Arthur loved when she did that. Her brown eyes matched her hair, and her full lips were almost always bare. She wore mascara and eyeliner, but lipstick rarely made the cut. And her red cheeks rendered rouge unnecessary. Her skin was pale, but her cheeks were crayon red at all times. When she laughed. When she was embarrassed. When she cried. Especially when she cried.

Arthur swallowed the rest of his beer in one drink and dropped a cigarette butt into the empty bottle. It sizzled and extinguished in a puff of smoke.

11:09 PM

Sarah shook her head, sinking deeper into the chair. "He's destroying himself."

Her father leaned against the doorframe, one hand in his pocket, the other massaging his beard.

"He's either on the phone or reading non-stop on the computer. That's when he's not working. And when he is working, he's doing the same thing between appointments. The place runs just fine without him there. He can afford some time away."

"It's his business, sweetheart. You know what that's like."

She reluctantly conceded. Sarah's father was a real estate broker; he lived in his button down shirt and slacks, car keys at his disposal any time the phone rang.

"But now? When I want him home? When I *need* him home." She looked down. "Maybe it's better anyway. When he's home, he's inconsolable. His mind, it just goes. Yeah, so does mine. It's always going. But his runs on a different speed, a different frequency."

"Hasn't it always been that way, hun?"

She grew frustrated with her father's perspective but knew he was right. It was something about Arthur that she had fallen in love with. That thickheaded, all-or-nothing mentality. It built their life to a comfortable standard. But now it infuriated her. "Yes. But I can't deal with it right now. It's too overwhelming." She sobbed.

"You can't just expect him to turn it off," said her father.

Whose side was he on? "I spend ninety-nine percent of my day trying to imagine where May might be," she said. "What she's doing. If she's *alive*." She choked the word from her mouth, her throat suddenly closing. "He's drinking so much. He screams and throws things. And I know he's trying his hardest, but every time I look at him, I'm crushed all over again." Her voice shot up an octave. "He doesn't look at me. He looks through me. He doesn't hold me." She dropped her forehead to the arm of the couch and hunched over, nearly limp, and sobbed so hard it sounded like hiccups, echoing in the quiet room.

Her father dropped quickly to his knee and placed an arm around her. She shifted and buried her face in his shoulder. "Daddy, where is she?" she wailed. His sweater muffled her cries. "Where is she?"

He pinched his eyes shut.

2.

Saturday, October 3, 2015, 11:03 AM

The shop television played a near-constant stream of local news. It was Saturday morning, and the front door of the tattoo parlor was wedged open, allowing the cool October morning air to circulate and waft away the previous day's scent. A man of about forty years, wearing a Philadelphia Eagles t-shirt and beaten up jeans, sauntered in and pulled off his baseball cap, displaying a receding hairline and a buzzed head. He waved as Arthur stood from behind the desk.

"Jake," the man said, reminding Arthur who he was. "I have an eleven AM appointment with you." He held out his hand.

"Right, Jake." Arthur shook firmly. "Sorry. Good to see you again. I think you'll like what I drew up for you." He walked back to the drawing desk on the left of the store and returned with a piece of paper. "What do you think?"

"Holy shit, man." Jake's eyes widened, his eyeballs bulging. "This is amazing."

Drawn in pristine black and white lines was the portrait of a bulldog, a tennis ball wedged in its mouth, drool oozing from its chops. In the background was a word-for-word scrawl of *Turn Again To Life* by Mary Lee Hall on a white piece of paper that was stressed and weathered at the edges. Arthur handed him back the original picture he had used for inspiration along with the copy of the poem.

"It's great," Jake said, still adoring the portrait. "I can't believe how much it looks like Fred."

"Let's get it on your back then! Come on to the chair. Hang out while I get set up."

The sun peered through the building's skylight, and a beam of light fell directly on the two of them. It was no coincidence – when you own the place, you get the best seat.

Dust particles reflecting in the bright sunlight snowed down with every movement. The rest of the room faded in contrast to the bright square of light around them. Arthur handed Jake the television remote. "Get comfortable, bud, gonna be awhile," he said. "Put on whatever you want." He loaded the tattoo machine with a fresh needle, slid the grip into place, tightened it, and then secured the needle with a few rubber bands doubled around the machine. He bagged the entire contraption in plastic, covering every millimeter aside from the very tip of the reservoir and the needle itself.

Jake took off his shirt and Arthur, using a disposable razor, shaved the patch of skin that would soon be on the receiving end of a permanent drawing. He wiped the area with disinfectant and transferred a stencil of the drawing onto Jake's back. He checked it from multiple angles to confirm the positioning was proper and directed Jake to a mirror to do the same. Upon confirmation, Arthur began filling ink caps with his choice of colors. Armed with a fresh paper towel sprayed with green soap in one hand and his machine in the other, he revved the needles.

"Two for one today: you get a tattoo of your best friend and you get rid of that Eagles t-shirt for a few hours."

"You're funny," said Jake. "Please don't tell me you're a goddamn Dallas fan."

"Jesus. Might as well make fun of my mother." Arthur dipped the machine in black ink, allowing some to collect in the reservoir. He was ready to outline. "New York Football Giants."

"Not from down here originally, are you? Or were you one of those kids who felt the need to be different from everyone in your family?"

"Born and raised in Bucks County," he said, drilling the top line of the dog's nose into Jake's skin. Jake didn't budge. "That good?" Given that the man was already covered in tattoos, he assumed he would be just fine, but Arthur always checked, regardless.

"Feels good. Where in Bucks?"

"Maplesville."

"No shit. I'm from Rockboro."

In the background, the television droned on with an incessant blur of drab stories interspersed with the occasional exuberant narrative thrown in for posterity. Arthur added line after line, connecting everything and completing the outline of the dog's nose. He wiped the excess ink, exposing his progress. "My pops was from North Jersey originally. Parsippany. He was a Giants and Mets fan."

He was making his way to the bulldog's eye, gracefully outlining the rippled face, when a warm sensation took him by the stomach. The warmth turned to heat, which sent a chill down his spine, and the heat turned to a ball of fire. All the while, he couldn't remove his gaze from the dog's unfinished eyes.

A commercial, its volume suddenly higher than the news broadcast, rose up over the noise of the machine. Arthur snapped out of his trance, bringing his attention back to Jake. "So, Fred was your dog?" He swallowed the extra spit gathering in his mouth. It tasted sour, and he felt as if he were going to vomit.

"Still is," said Jake. "He's eight."

It wasn't often that someone wanted a memorial tattoo of something that was still alive. Arthur was relieved.

"Fred got me through some fucked up stuff. I was in a bad place for a long time. Living out of my car, you know, a big sob story. But Fred kept me company, kept my spirits up. I had a really shitty epiphany a few weeks back that Fred is likely in the twilight of his life. It shook me up. Full-blown panic attack ensued; I cried like a toddler for an hour. My girlfriend showed me this poem that was her grandmother's favorite. Her grandfather had given it to his wife when he was diagnosed with cancer. Became their mantra, sort of. It got them through a rough time. He recovered and lived another two decades. But they still looked to it when things got rough. As soon as I read it, it instantly made me feel better. The dread lifted a bit. I figured I'd enjoy whatever time I have left with him."

"We all end in the ocean," Arthur recited.

"You got that right."

Arthur swallowed hard and grimaced. "You should've brought the big guy in. Would've been fun to meet him."

"I'll bring him by one day when I'm out for a walk. He's even uglier in person."

The laugh held the burning at bay for a moment but, by now, the hairs on the back of Arthur's neck were standing on end. "I have to take a leak," he lied. He pulled off his gloves and stood up. "Should've done that before starting. Too much iced tea."

He closed the bathroom door behind him and splashed cold water onto his face. The cramped room felt comfortable, cradling him as he stared at his reflection in the mirror. The person who returned the gaze was a sorry excuse for Arthur Parish. This was a zombie. His normally taught skin was loose and oily with heavy, black bags pulling on the lower eyelids. The lower half of his face was covered in stubble, and his hair, slicked straight back, boasted grays at the sides that he didn't remember being there in the morning. Maybe that was yesterday morning. He couldn't recall the last time he'd even looked in a mirror.

Snap out of it. Work to do.

He washed his hands and returned to Jake.

"Sorry about that."

"I pee at least five dozen times a day," Jake said. "Too much Gatorade. I drink the stuff like it's actually nutritious."

"You running marathons?" Arthur asked, snapping on a new pair of gloves and lifting his machine from the table. He continued where he left off.

"Yeah," Jake said, patting his stomach. "Tons."

The hypnotizing, swirling heat resumed almost as quickly as the buzzing needles. Arthur fought through it. "So how long have you been with your girlfriend?" he asked, clearing his throat twice, harder the second time.

"About three years." Jake stopped fiddling with his phone. "We met the day I got out of rehab. I was eating a burger in town and she sat next to me with her bulldog. Showed her pictures of mine. We went to the dog park the next day. Rest is history." Jake leaned comfortably against the synthetic leather seat which had been adjusted to give Arthur the best angle for the tattoo. He stared out the front door. New Hope foot traffic was hustling and bustling, as it was any Saturday that wasn't a blizzard. Sometimes even then. "What about you? Married?"

Arthur unconsciously rubbed his gloved thumb against the ring on his left hand. He could feel it through the nitrile. "Yeah. Yeah, I'm married. A little over eight years now." He pursed his lips.

"Ah, that's nice, man. I'm planning on asking my lady to marry me in a few months. Actually ring shopping with her mother tomorrow. Marriage is the best. Constantly being around someone you love, what more can you ask for, you know?" He belly laughed. It was a jolly sound, but it jarred Arthur. "You guys want kids?"

The heat spilled over, radiating outward into his arms and legs. He closed his eyes. "We have a daughter." The vibration of the machine in his hand was too much. He eased his foot off the pedal just as a bead of sweat trickled down the side of his face and then wiped the excess ink from Jake's back. "She'll turn one next month."

"That's sweet."

"Yeah," Arthur said, depressing the pedal again. "Yeah, it's the best."

A woman's face on the television caught his attention. He knew it from somewhere, an actress perhaps. Red, curly hair, dangling in springs, stretched far below her shoulders. He fought with his cloudy brain to place her. A movie he'd seen recently. Yes.

Only that couldn't be it. She was standing in front of a house – her own? A little girl, likely the woman's daughter from the way the woman wrapped her arms around the child, stood next to her. Arthur released the pedal.

"Codi," he said aloud.

"Scuse me?"

"The girl on TV." Arthur motioned blankly to the mounted television even though Jake couldn't see him from his angle. "I tattooed her," he said. "A few months back. She was in here. Her daughter was missing."

"Whoa. I guess they got her back."

"The … the cops had all but given up," Arthur said incredulously, shaking his head, still staring at the television.

The woman hugged the little girl, squeezed her, unwilling to let go. Cara, Arthur remembered. She looked like Codi. The same coiled hair and smattering of freckles. She looked up at her mother with eyes so bright and content that they glowed in the daylight. Codi returned the gaze, smiling ear to ear, and squeezed the child against her. They were cheek to cheek.

The clip cut to a shot of them on their lawn. Codi tickled Cara. Both laughed so hard their faces turned red.

Arthur's own eyes widened and his mouth hung on a hinge. A banner materialized on the bottom of the screen:

FOLLOW UP: Mother and Daughter, Six Months After Being Reunited

"Isn't that something?" Jake said. "Thank God. How often does that happen?"

Arthur's closed his eyes and tears spurted from the corners of them.

"Hey, you all right, man?" asked Jake.

Arthur nodded. "Just happy for her."

11:39 AM

"Come on, sweetie, the lady wants to talk to us again."

Cara obeyed her mother. They stood at the foot of their driveway, Cara hanging on to Codi's leg for dear life, grinning the entire time.

The reporter gave her cameraman the thumbs up and stood before the two of them, her microphone up to her mouth. "It's obvious that you are both still ecstatic. The look in your eyes says it all. What have the last six months been like?" She extended the microphone to Codi's mouth.

Codi shook her head and wiped her eyes with the back of her sleeve. "A dream come true. There are nights I still wake up looking for her. Knowing she's in her bed, safe and sound, there's nothing like it. The hell I went through for all that time, it's the opposite. It's even better. You can't put it into words."

"Unquantifiable," the reporter suggested.

"Yes." Codi smiled at Cara.

"And your daughter – she certainly looks content."

"She's happy to be with Mommy. Right, baby?" Codi asked. Cara only smiled.

"Thank you," said the reporter. She turned to face the camera. "We're glad we came to visit Codi and Cara; however, not all stories have such happy endings. Remember, if you know something, say something. I'm Michelle Young ..."

That night, as the hint of a fall breeze eddied through the still-green trees, Cara snuggled into the corner of the couch, holding her tablet and playing games. Codi flitted about the kitchen, cleaning and tidying as she went, the day's dinner eaten and the dishes done. Her parents sat on the loveseat, their place for the last thirty years. The sofa itself had changed multiple times, but its contents remained the same: Dad doing a crossword puzzle, television remote in hand or close by, Mom reading a book (likely a thriller but occasionally a romance novel). It was during those times that, even at the ripe age of seventy, they'd sit a little closer and hands would wander, first from Mom's side, then from Dad, once he got the hint. Oblivious at a young age and repulsed once she became aware, Codi now found it somewhat charming, especially given that they were oblivious to her catching on.

Codi washed her hands in the bathroom next to the kitchen. She studied herself in the medicine cabinet mirror as she scrubbed, finding her face a bit fuller. She had a tranquility about her now that wasn't there even after Cara had been returned home only a few short months ago. Anxiety doesn't just end like a song – it reverberates through your being, shaking you long after the worst of it is over, like an aftershock. Things were almost normal again and normalcy was important to Codi. Reestablishing their life schedule meant doing things the way they used to do them, like it or not. And at first, she didn't like it. It took a strong woman and Codi was strong – stronger now after the ordeal, even if at times she thought she wasn't, and even when Xanax pills, scattered across her parents' granite countertops as she hastily opened and then dropped the bottle, seemed like the only option. But watching Cara sleeping peacefully in her bed, more relaxed as the nights went by, throttled the anxiety. Slowly but steadily, the perversion in their lives seemed to fade.

In her reflection, Codi also noticed lines around her eyes and carved into her forehead that had not been there before. *Scars*, she thought. Scars that would eventually deepen, no matter the cocktail of lotions and salves and beauty supplies she buttered on them. Vanity was a complex of everyone, and she was no different. But the scars were worth it.

What would she have done if her daughter had not been returned that Sunday morning, six months ago? If they'd found Cara's body in a ditch, caked in mud and clumps of dead leaves from the winter runoff? If what the crazy homeless guy had said hadn't been true?

She would have killed herself. She had the gun in the drawer next to her bed. Her friend Davey gave it to her in the nights following the kidnapping, when she refused to stay away from the house in case Cara came home. They called her crazy. Toddlers don't just stumble home, they said. The last laugh was hers, but there had been no one left to tell *I told you so.* Everything and everyone else outside of Cara was irrelevant. Still, the thoughts crept in and out of her mind like a nosy neighbor. The neighbor who knows what package has been delivered before you even get home from work.

How long would it have been before she blew her own brains across her single-occupancy, queen-size bed? The only thing she had to go on was the hope she had been given when he, the man wearing nothing but jeans cut into shorts, a green t-shirt, a beard braided to his chest, and old, spit-and-dirt-encrusted Chuck Taylors who went by the name of John Braun, told her what she would need to do to see her daughter again. He had no involvement, let that be known, and he would repeat that over and over again just to be sure. He could *not* be arrested again. No siree! He would not be harassed by the local police, the ones who had always had it out for him. No, he was only there to tell her the story. No blood on his hands. He didn't always believe in a heaven, but he was not taking any chances. After all life had handed him, he deserved a heaven. And though he was dealt a shitty hand, and though it might've been easier on those who had to feast their eyes on the decay of society, he could not die. Not yet. He needed to stay alive, if only to feed his snorting and dirtier-than-scum bulldog and, of course, to be there for those in Codi's position. His words, verbatim. Codi could recite them in her sleep, and sometimes did, mumbled and garbled, looping around somewhere in the anxious, half-sedated state in which she would briefly rest while her child was off somewhere, with someone else. Something about that man's words stuck to her like a magnet. And the harder she tried to disregard it, the more believable and real it felt. So she accepted it – finally *admitted* she accepted it. Really, it was part of her long before her date with John Braun in Crux, Pennsylvania. Long before the homeless man and the filthy old dog made her question everything about life and how it worked. It was part of her the moment she stepped foot on the cursed grounds around Vance State Park.

"Mama, tee-vee!" a small voice announced from the living room.

The entire family had been waiting for the re-airing of their news segment so Cara could watch herself on television. "Coming, baby." She dried her hands on the hanging towel and shut off the light.

"Look, look!" Cara squawked as Codi returned to the living room. "It's Mama and Cawwa!" She hopped up and down on the couch, the cushions huge under her tiny body. Her size was more apparent than ever to Codi, her fragility strikingly obvious.

"It is, Cara! Look at you!" she pointed. Codi's parents sat forward on their loveseat, grins on their faces.

"On tee-vee!" Cara yelled again while squeezing Codi's cheeks with her hands and staring at herself on the television set. She prodded and rubbed them without paying attention, her fingers tensing with excitement.

"*We're glad we came to visit Codi and Cara; however, not all stories have such happy endings. Remember, if you know something, say something. I'm Michelle Young for WPIC.*"

"Over!" Cara said, hopping up and down again on the big cushion.

"Okay, sweetheart, time for bed! I let you stay up to watch it, now we need to get some much-needed sleep!"

Cara giggled, spoke some gibberish, and fell onto her side in the middle of the couch, feigning sleep with a loud snore.

"You taped it?" asked Mother. "Cindy wants to see it when she comes over tomorrow night."

"Uh huh," Codi said vacantly. Her eyes were following the slideshow montage of missing children that the news was airing after the segment. Each slide displayed a few seconds at a time, a picture superimposed on a black background, the name and year of each child missing in bold white font underneath. Codi's heart sank as they cycled one by one.

"Poor souls," said Mother. "Each one of them has a parent going through exactly what you went through. What a shame."

"Where's the remote?" Codi asked abruptly. She searched the couch and coffee table with her eyes.

"I have it," Dad said. He held it out.

Codi skipped back thirty seconds, waited a few slides, and gasped. She skipped back again, this time pausing it on a particular image, a man holding a baby while the mother hovered next to them. Underneath, in the same white font, *May Parish. April 2015.*

"What's wrong?" Dad asked.

"I know him," she said as she rubbed her ribs. She stared long at the image on the screen. "And I know where his baby is."

3.

Saturday, October 3, 2015, 10:14 PM

A bar is a house of voices. Voices heard and unheard, voices in distress, voices of hope and love, and hate. New voices. Old voices. New voices meeting old voices. Fighting, violent voices. Rejected voices. Elated voices. A bar is the church of the common man when church isn't for the common man. Or when the common man isn't for the church. The Paunched Pig was a good bar. It didn't always house good voices, but neither did a confessional.

Arthur's voice was small, trampled but not defeated. It was still calculated, but no longer wasting of words. And he certainly no longer minced them.

"Fuck you, Greg."

Greg stood from his stool.

"Not in here," Pete said sternly, a pint glass in hand, the tap spouting suds into it.

"I'm just sick of his goddamn attitude, Pete," said

Arthur. "If you've got something to say, come over here and say it."

"My attitude? I didn't say anything to you."

"You're right. You said it *at* me. You think I'm fucking dumb, Greg? No one ever calls you out. Here you go, asshole, you got your wish."

Pete raised his voice. "I said enough. Go outside if you guys want to get tough."

"Tell this guy to leave me the hell alone, then," Arthur said. "Every night he opens his big fucking mouth, spouting off about why this town is going downhill. Everyone's a problem except Greg. Always been that way, right Greg?"

Greg stared at Arthur, still standing.

"First it was the faggots, now it's the tattoos. What about when you came into my shop for a quote? Or the fact that I tattooed your sister. She told me how much of a prick you were, too."

Greg moved forward. Two of his friends stood and stepped in front of him. Arthur hopped off his stool, which wobbled but righted itself. Standing was easier than he thought – not enough alcohol to make him woozy yet, just enough to rid himself of a few inhibitions.

Greg and his friends were the townies, asses glued to the same seats every night. It had been that way since a few years out of high school. Everyone knew their names, even ten years and forty pounds later. Arthur picked them out the first night he, Alejandro, and Mason sat for a beer after the shop's grand opening, four years earlier.

They're easy to spot. They sit, forearms on the bar and hunched over their drinks like it's their kitchen, most still wearing work clothes. They yell instead of talk, and laugh even louder, wanting the entire world to hear what they have to say. It's their town. They smirk and mutter things to one another while staring at the patrons around them. Everyone is fair game.

Arthur observed, as he did for most of his life. Being aware of his surroundings was important, an escape plan always necessary. He was particularly protective of Sarah. He would take her to the Pig often before they had May. Greg was always there, sometimes cordial, sometimes drunk, but always staring. Always raping her with his eyes.

With never more than a beer or two in his system, and without the rage he now possessed, Arthur had no intentions beyond nodding, keeping it cordial. After all, he didn't want to have to avoid coming to the Pig. It was around the corner from work, and a nice place to boot. So what if Greg stared? Let him have his fun. He couldn't land tail like Sarah if he added six inches. Be proud. Wrap your arm around her – even if you want to break his face.

"What's the matter, Greg? With all the shit-talking you do, I'm shocked you can't handle it. You know I'm sitting right here, so what? Would you prefer I sit here and eat your shit while you talk? No one else will say anything to you. Well here you go, Greg. That's all it takes for you to peel your ass off that stool?"

Greg pushed through his friends, and Arthur balled his fists. He widened his stance, bracing for what would undoubtedly be a lot more weight than he could handle. As Greg closed in, Arthur cocked back, hoping to move out of the way and crack him in the side of the head. Maybe Greg's momentum would keep him moving and he'd wipeout on the stools. But Arthur felt someone grab him, and it wasn't Greg. It was a blur at first. Then it was a figure. Someone bigger than Greg. The person stopped Greg in his tracks with one arm and turned to hold Arthur the same way.

"That'll be all, gentlemen. Greg, go sit down." The man turned to face Arthur. It was Simon Shelley. He smirked and shook his head. "You got a death wish, Arthur?"

Greg shook his head and sat down. "Damn did you luck out, Arthur. I wouldn't be talking so much shit if I were you."

"Eat a dick."

"Keep going. We'll see what happens next time a cop doesn't save your ass."

"Thatch, shut up," Shelley warned. "You're not going to do anything but sit there and have your drink. It's over."

"Tell *him*, Shelley," Greg said. "I was minding my own business."

Shelley nudged Arthur over to a table in the corner of the dining room. He was strong, effortlessly moving Arthur where he wanted. Arthur didn't put up a fight. "Come on. Come sit," Shelley said. He pulled out a chair and plopped down across from Arthur. "You all right? You're gonna get yourself hurt, man. You have to calm down."

"Fuck him," said Arthur. "I'm tired of his shit, and I'm not in the mood to deal with it."

"I can tell."

Pete walked over. "You okay?"

Arthur nodded dismissively.

"You know I can't have that in here. Greg is a prick. Leave him be. He's been coming here forever, and he's harmless."

Arthur cackled, spinning a cardboard coaster on the black-painted wooden table. "Harmless."

"Simon, you want a Guinness?"

Shelley nodded. "Please. Can I get an order of the sliders too? Arthur, you want something?"

"No. Thanks." He spat nails. "Actually, Pete, bring me another one."

Pete patted Arthur on his shoulder, then strolled away. A moment later, he returned with Arthur's half-empty pint. Arthur nodded. He drained the drink and looked up at Shelley. "Thanks for stepping in."

The Pig was an Irish Pub, with dark walls, tables, and chairs. The music was mostly traditional Celtic with some punk mixed in. Depending on the day of the week, contemporary hits were played, but they tended to stay true to the theme and heritage. Because it attracted locals as well as tourists, it felt authentic. Arthur found solace in that, even if he only pretended to know his Irish ancestry.

Pete dropped off the two beers.

"Haven't seen you here in a while," Arthur said to Shelley.

"It's been a little crazy at work."

"A little." Arthur smiled without much humor. "It's a little crazy everywhere. You called Greg a different name before."

"Graduated high school with him. His last name is Thatcher. We called him Thatch because he liked it. He called us by our last name too, but I always hated being called Shelley, for obvious reasons. Especially in high school. Funny, now it's how people know me. Anyway, he used to shotgun beers by the case. Not really much of a surprise there. Then again, so did I. I'd like to think I'm not too much of a dick."

"It's less the shotgunning of beer and more the being a dick that makes him a dick."

Simon raised his eyebrows and shrugged before drinking from his beer. His blue eyes, wide and alert at all times, closed for a minute as he drank, enjoying his treat after a long shift. "Sometimes this place gets me through the day, you know? Looking forward to something." The pint glass looked small in his hand. His arms stressed the inside of his t-shirt. He carried the air of a police officer, minus some of the characteristic abrasiveness. At least, he didn't seem to bring it home with him.

"I know what you mean." Arthur drank from his new pint, gulping down much more than Simon in his first sip.

Simon dropped his head a few inches. "I'm sorry. I don't mean to complain, you know?"

Arthur shook his head.

"How are you doing?"

"Shitty. I hate everyone. I hate everything. I hate this beer. I hate you. I hate myself." He drank again. "I was never this way. I didn't get into bar fights, like some fucking townie. Not my style. I'm just angry *all the time*. And I don't think it has anything to do with May. It's Sarah."

"Your wife."

"Yeah. My ex-wife, I guess. That sounds odd."

"Chief told me that you guys weren't together. I guess the detectives told him. This case has hit the station hard. Most of us have never experienced anything like it, aside from a few senior guys, but they don't really talk about it. They go over this stuff in the academy, which was like a hundred years ago already, but nothing prepares you for it."

"I'm sure the statistics don't help matters."

Simon looked at his beer. The clamoring of patrons wasn't as obvious now.

"I've read it all, man." Arthur said. "Trust me. There's nothing in your head that I haven't seen or heard yet. No evidence, no suspects, no witnesses. The fact that she's not been seen anywhere. All signs point to *not good*." He drank more. "The fucked up part of it all is that I truly believe she's alive. As crazy as that sounds. It just doesn't make sense. I spent six months thinking she was dead, and I kept hope. I did all I could. Now something flips the switch in my head to *fuck it all* and suddenly I get this attack of optimism. I don't know what to feel anymore."

"Have you gone to see anyone?"

"Like a shrink?"

"Nah, not necessarily. There are other people. Psychologists. Even a friend. Just someone to vent to. It's important."

"I tried that with Sarah and she took off on me," he said, laughing.

"Do the two of you still speak?" Simon asked.

"Only when she calls. She doesn't answer the phone when I dial her. So that just leads to me tearing her a new asshole when I finally talk to her. Then she hangs up on me. It's counterproductive, but I can't hear her voice without wanting to slap her. God knows I'd never do that. At least, I don't think I would. But she's pushing buttons, you know? In her own head she's right. To her, I'm a shell of who I was, and she couldn't take it anymore. Her words. And I can even justify it, sometimes. But for worse or for better, right? I'm taking all this on my back. For the both of us. The least she could do is understand."

"I hear that," said Simon.

"You married?"

"I was."

"Went to shit too?"

"Ten years in," said Shelley. "I screwed around, didn't get caught. Screwed around again, didn't get caught. Thought I was invincible. I was a good father, provided for my son, took care of the family. I treated her like a queen. We went on vacations all over the place. I gave them everything, but I got careless. She hit me with the papers. I thought it would go away and she'd forgive and forget. But she didn't, and I didn't have a leg to stand on. I don't see my son as much as I'd like to anymore, but I'm still there as often as possible. His mom and I aren't friendly. So half the time I'm fighting her, and then I get frustrated and give up and it affects the kid. And then it looks like I'm not there for him."

"Jesus. It's all fucked up, isn't it?" Arthur asked, looking around.

Simon cleared his throat, his voice hesitating. "You know," he paused, "I call him every night now. Since the night your daughter …" He cracked his knuckles with one hand. "I just appreciate him a little more now, I think. Not that I didn't before. But sometimes you don't realize how blessed you are."

Pete dropped off the sliders. "You good, Arthur?"

"Yeah." Arthur hacked out a laugh. "Sorry, Pete," he said quietly.

Pete rolled his eyes. "Thought we might need the cops. Then Simon rolled in, and I still thought we might need the cops."

Simon flipped Pete the finger.

"Enjoy, guys."

Arthur waited for Pete to leave. "So, that's why you never hang up on me when I call every day." He chuckled.

Simon looked up from his food. "You know there isn't much I can do or tell you. But you can call whenever you need to."

"Thank you."

Simon pulled out his phone. "What's your number? I'll text you so you can put me in your contacts. Don't worry about calling the station. Just buzz me if you need something."

Arthur did as he was told. "We've known each other, what, four or five years? This is the first time I'm having a beer with you."

"Hey, better late than never." They clinked glasses and Simon finished one of the sliders while Arthur finished his drink.

Sunday, October 4, 2015, 3:03 AM

Arthur tossed and turned in his bed. It was a king-size and, even though Sarah hadn't been there in almost a month, her side remained nearly as neat and orderly as the day she left. The top sheet was tucked in, the blanket folded back perfectly. He should've known something was up – she never made the bed.

He slept above the covers. October hadn't quite given way to air cold enough to warrant a comforter. That, and he often collapsed as drunk as possible in a heap on his side, never earlier than two or three in the morning. He'd sleep like he were dead, provided he'd had enough to drink, and then spring to life bright and early, like clockwork.

Tonight was no different – rife with memories and violent, antagonizing thoughts. They came like a freight train and were just as loud, buzzing in his ears enough to make him wince.

He pictured Sarah sleeping peacefully in her old bedroom at her parents' house. Was she even thinking of May? Did May exist to her anymore? *Selfish bitch* ...

He fell asleep at the thought, and then woke a few seconds later.

... She wasn't always like this. She was never like this. Who would have thought it would end this way?

Freshman year of college, during the first week of classes, when they were both away from their family for the first time, lonely and tentative, a magnetism attracted them to each other in the library. They had calculus class together; Arthur was proficient, and Sarah was quite the mathematical dunce. After she left his bed the next morning, he was sure he had ignited a potential college sex career that would span all four years. A serious affair was the last thing he wanted after coming out of a long and broken high school relationship, far too advanced and serious for his years. But when she showed up at his dorm room that very night with Chinese takeout and her calculus textbook, there wasn't much to do but give in. In retrospect, to Arthur, it was all too desperate. She didn't know him, aside from his naked body, yet he fell in love because of her desperation. He loved her because she loved him blindly.

He fell out cold again, but most of the beer had run its course and his eyelids flashed open again half an hour later, long enough that the crusted tears in the corners of his eyes stung his skin as they pulled open.

... I should've killed Greg tonight. I should've picked up my stool and stabbed the leg through his fucking face. How could someone who knows my situation be such a ...

And, finally, he was gone for the night.

Monday, October 5, 2015, 5:12 PM

Codi stared at Sarah from across the lobby. The roar of a few-dozen office jockeys, hungry for freedom, cluttered the air. Her view was obstructed at times, and she moved her head back and forth in order to keep a close eye on Sarah, who had stopped at a vending machine on her way out of the building. Once outside, Codi walked up beside her.

"Sarah?"

Sarah looked over, startled. She put her hand on her chest and smiled. "Yeah?"

"Sorry, I didn't mean to creep up on you like that. It gets so nuts in there."

"It's no problem, I just didn't expect it. Codi, right?"

"I'm impressed you remembered my name," Codi said. Unprompted, they both started walking away from the building.

"You're in customer service, yeah?" asked Sarah. "We met at the outing at Vance last year, right? You had your daughter with you."

"Yes!" *And you were pregnant,* she thought. *Tiny little thing. Could barely tell. Barely.* "You're in technical writing."

"I am. You're …?"

"HR."

"Right."

The stretch of sidewalk wrapped around the side of the building, where it opened to a parking lot that had been freshly tarred less than a week before and the smell still lingered in the air. It reminded Codi of summer. They walked past her car, unbeknownst to Sarah.

"I think I know where your daughter is."

Sarah snapped her head around, facing Codi straight on. Any hint of cordiality flushed from her face, replaced by a pale pallor. Her bag fell from her fingertips to the ground, toppling to its side. "What did you just say?" she asked in a tiny voice.

Codi, stony-faced, took Sarah by her hand, cradling it in her own. "I need you to listen to me carefully."

"Who are you?" Sarah asked, yanking her hand away.

"I'm a mom who went through what you're going through now. My daughter went missing a year ago."

Sarah wiped away a tear with the sleeve of her

navy blue sweater, which was pulled over a white, button-down shirt, the collar folded over. A locket hung from her neck. She unconsciously grabbed it with her free hand. "What does that have to do with May? Where is she? Please tell me. Why would you do it? Why? She's a baby." Her voice shuddered and broke with every word.

"I didn't do it, sweetheart." Now Codi broke down. "Not purposely."

The words struck Codi like a mallet to her spine. Her hands and fingers tingled and her knees turned to rubber. "Stop fucking with me." She shook her head. "I don't deserve this. Who put you up to this? Who told you to do this?" She pulled both of her hands to her chest and leaned against the door of the car behind her.

"This isn't a joke. I wish it were. I'm here to help you."

"You're a miserable person!" Sarah growled, raising her voice for the first time. She picked up her bag and dashed toward her car.

"Sarah," Codi said from behind her. The sun peeked from behind a cloud and the day brightened like someone had flicked a light switch. The winds of fall had suddenly crept over the region but in the direct sun it was still warm. Codi felt the heat on the side of her body. "Your husband is Arthur. The tattoo artist. He gave me this." She lifted her shirt past her ribs.

Sarah didn't turn around. Instead, she unlocked

her car door with the remote and pulled it open.

"She just disappeared, didn't she?"

Sarah froze.

Codi pulled her shirt back down. "Into thin air. Abracadabra, gone. From right under your nose. No footprints or fingerprints. Nothing."

Sarah remained facing the inside of her car, her hands trembling. She breathed hard, having to remind herself. Her shoulders rose and settled with each deliberate breath. "How do you know that?"

"Because the same thing happened to me." Codi moved closer as Sarah turned to face her. "My daughter disappeared from her bed while I was in the next room. While my parents were in the living room downstairs. No TVs on. No music. Silence. There were no footsteps. Nothing out of place. There was a bang. Then screaming and hollering." She reached out for Sarah's shoulder.

Sarah shuddered. "Don't touch me." She cringed away.

Codi shook her head. "Sarah …"

Sarah got into her car and slammed the door, panicking, not taking her eyes off Codi.

"Why are you doing this? Let me explain! I can tell you everything you need to know! I can help you!"

Sarah reversed out of her spot, tires squealing, and pulled her phone from the top of her purse.

"Don't call the police, Sarah!" Codi yelled. She looked around. "You'll make it worse!" she shouted as the car sped away.

5:18 PM

Arthur dragged on the cigarette, burning it down to the filter, past the warning line. He inhaled, pulling in the surrounding smoke that curled around his mouth and fingers. It came out in a cloud, thinner and lighter than it had gone in, and dispersed around him. The fog around his body drifted slowly through the window and out into the atmosphere.

The sun was setting, and the colors of dusk were just starting to illuminate as the clouds began to part for the first time all day. The street glimmered with beads of water, luminescent in the waning light. The smell, once comforting, meant nothing to Arthur, and he leaned his chin on his hand on the ledge of the window. He closed his eyes and started to doze when something rang. At first, the sound seemed to be coming from far off in the distance, but as lucidity came to him, he realized it was the phone right next to his head.

Sarah.

The hell did she want? *Now* she was ready to talk. At her leisure, of course. She could wait. She could wait a long time. The opportunity to turn the tables had come, and Arthur was going to take it.

It rang a third time.

But what if it were pertaining to May? No, Simon would call him first, he thought. But Simon wasn't on the case – Detective Reed was their contact. And he'd seemingly called Sarah first with anything related to the case, likely a coincidence at first and a habit at this point. Calling the mom of the child wasn't terribly surprising.

It rang a fourth time.

Maybe this isn't a good time to be playing games, he thought. He swiped just in time – another second would have sent the call to voicemail.

"Sarah." Her name came out softer than he had intended. Desperate. Missing her. "What's up?" he asked, making his voice much sterner.

She was whimpering.

"Arthur, some crazy woman that I work with told me she knows where May is. She ... she said she didn't do it on purpose. She admitted she did it." Sarah was crazed, the words coming out in a garbled mess. *"But she said she didn't really do it. I didn't believe her ... I ... I don't believe her ..."*

"Sarah-"

"I don't think I believe her ..."

"Sarah, slow down," he said. "I can barely understand what you're saying." He got up from the chair and paced the bedroom.

"This girl, Codi ..."

He stopped in his tracks.

"... she said that she knows ... she thinks she knows where May is. She knew about the house and how she just disappeared and that nothing was missing and the bang, she mentioned the bang and the screaming."

"Okay, where is she now? Can you put her on the phone?"

"I left! I drove away! She was scaring the shit out of me!"

Arthur shook his head. "Okay, can you turn around? Is she still there?"

"I'm on 202 already. I'm not going back. I'll call the police."

"Don't!" he yelled and nearly dropped the phone, catching it between his neck and shoulder. "Just don't. I know where she lives. I'll go see her."

"Arthur, what the hell? No."

"Sarah, trust me."

"If she's not lying, this could be our chance at finding May. Or something we could use at the very least. Why would you want to fuck that up, Arthur? No, I'm going to the police. Because even if she's lying, I want to get her for it. She can't get away with this." She paused briefly. *"And how the fuck do you know her?"*

Hearing her swear so heavily was unnerving.

"Arthur, are you there?"

"I think I tattooed her."

"Do you want to call them or do you want me to?"

He thought a minute. "Drive here."

"What?"

"Drive down here. Come to the house."

There was silence on the other end of the line.

"Sarah?"

"Okay."

"Okay?"

"I'll be there soon."

5:47 PM

Arthur plopped onto the couch. A plume of dust coughed out around him. The living room hadn't been used much in the last seven months.

He stared at the playpen, folded against the side of the fireplace since the night May disappeared. The rocking horse, painted three shades of pink with a mane of yarn and M-A-Y stenciled onto the saddle, hadn't been rocked. He clasped his hands in his lap and crossed one leg over the other, flapping his foot up and down and drumming his thumbs on his legs.

How he missed them both terribly.

He closed his eyes and they burned. He had not seen his wife in a month, had not even spoken with her for the last few weeks beyond a text message he sent saying "I love you," which might as well have been sent into space.

Headlights beamed through the front window. He felt a hint of anger rumbling in his gut and up into his chest as he heard the car pull into the driveway. He suppressed it, swallowing it back down, keeping it where it needed to be for the time being, and got up to meet her at the door just as she cut the engine and the headlights.

She approached the house and he stood before her, scraggly, gaunt, and beaten. The subtle, sad smile on his face concealed none of it. His eyes were sunken, his cheekbones prominent. He'd shaven at one point or another in the last few weeks, so the facial hair wasn't quite a beard, but it was overgrown. His t-shirt hung on his shoulders like it were still hanging in the closet. She started to cry, and he knew from her face that his appearance alarmed her.

Even stressed and tired, she was as beautiful as ever, albeit a little too skinny herself. He walked down the two brick steps and pulled her into his arms. She wrapped herself around his waist.

"I've missed you," he said into her ear.

4.

Monday, October 5, 2015, 6:05 PM

Arthur drank long from the bottle. The water guzzled from the opening as air escaped the suction of his lips.

Sarah took a sip from hers.

"Her daughter went missing in August of 2014," he said. He put the plastic bottle down on the countertop and leaned back against the refrigerator, crossing his arms. "I spent almost four hours with her. Tattooed a giraffe onto her ribs, which is her daughter's favorite animal, along with Cara's name next to it."

"Cara's her name?"

He nodded. "Seeing her on the television sent my day into a tailspin. I couldn't stop thinking about it, how similar it was, from what I could remember, at least. I was wondering if I might've embellished a bit. I don't know. I *wanted* it to be the same. I mean, she *found* her daughter."

"After eight months," said Sarah. She stared longingly into the distance, her elbows on her knees and her body leaning forward.

Arthur nodded. "Maybe she can help us."

Sarah shook her head. "Do you really think this is related? Thousands of kids are taken every year. From their homes. From stores. Cars. School. Everywhere. Plenty of sickos and prey everywhere."

"Right, but this similarly? Gone without a trace? No fingerprints? Nothing disturbed? We already knew something wasn't right, Sarah. That's obvious. Whether you admit it or not, you know that something's off about all of it."

Sarah lifted her eyebrows. "But to trust a person I don't know? A person who apparently had all the knowledge about May when we had barely spoken more than a cordial, small-talking hello at any point in however long we've worked together? Hell, I've never even been to her department."

"All I want to do is talk to her. Call it a hunch."

"I can't go on a hunch," said Sarah. "This is our daughter's life."

"Then listen to what I'm trying to say."

"I have been listening, but we can't do it this way. What if she's the one who took May? Or what if, at the very least, she's a part of it? She used the words 'Not purposely.' If she's telling the truth, she was involved. No one just says these things for fun. And if she is fucking around, and has gone to these great lengths of finding out all the information just to play some cruel joke, then she's out of her goddamned mind anyway. And is that really someone we want to mess around with?"

Arthur walked silently from his place against the refrigerator to the window behind the sink. Dishes and silverware from his lunch were submerged in soapy water in a pot. "Maybe she's simply trying to help," he finally said, facing the window.

"What is it about her, Arthur? Are you in love with this woman or something?"

The question stung.

"We've worked so close with Detective Reed, why this now? Why not trust them to do their jobs?"

"Because it doesn't add up." He turned to face her, brooding, his eyes bloodshot, his voice remaining even. "Why would she wait this long if she were really at fault?"

"Guilt?"

"Then wouldn't she go to the police?" he asked.

"Would you?"

"Look, she stumbled into my tattoo shop. Had no idea who I was. Is it a really fantastic coincidence?" he asked. "Maybe we're just lucky that she happened to be in town that day. But I spent four hours with her, and I just can't help but to believe that this isn't some elaborate plan to kidnap our child. That's asinine. For what? Did she demand money? Is she looking for something out of it?" He pulled a chair from underneath the table and sat on it, scooting closer to

Sarah. He leaned in. "She may know things she doesn't want to tell the police, things that could implicate her or her daughter. She just got her kid back. She's not looking to put that in jeopardy. If we go in there and tell them what she knows about us and that we think she's involved, we're going to destroy her life."

There was no remorse on Sarah's face.

"And on top of that, she may clam up. Might tell them she doesn't know anything and just thought she could help because she read the story and … and it was similar to her own. She came right to you. She obviously cares enough to do that, right? If we go and fuck it up by telling the police, and they bring her in and she gets the story wrong, we could cost ourselves a chance at May."

"What if we do that by not going to them?" she asked.

Arthur ran his tongue along the inside of his teeth. "I know this is the right way."

"Arthur, was May born yet when this girl …"

"Codi."

"… When Codi came in for a tattoo?"

"Yes."

Sarah smiled as if she'd already proven her point. It wasn't her normal, perky smile. It was callous and sarcastic. "Did you tell her where we lived? Show her pictures?"

"I don't tell anyone where we live. Where *I* live. And yes, I showed her a picture of May. She was a month old. I showed her a picture of a bald lump of cute flesh with barely a distinguishing feature from every other bald lump of cute flesh on earth."

"I'm not talking about picking May out of a lineup. I'm talking about emotions, Arthur. Push a fucking baby out of your vagina and you'll understand what seeing one does to a woman. Then take her baby away and see how she reacts. We cry and miss our children being in our body when they're *right in front of us*. This woman gets her heart ripped out of her chest and then you show her a picture of your newborn."

"She seemed to have so much hope when she was in the shop." Arthur spoke as if he'd already been defeated.

"No one ever thinks …"

They both paused.

"I don't know," said Arthur. "I haven't given up, Sarah."

"You look like you have."

He looked away. "I haven't. I *haven't*. Especially not recently. I've just had this feeling like she's … okay."

Sarah sighed. "What if she took May? What if she took May and she found her kid and ended up stuck with a child who isn't hers, hidden somewhere? And now she feels guilty and wants to give May back to us."

"Even more of a reason not to get anyone else involved. If that's the case, and I truly don't believe it, then we get May back safely. We worry about the rest after. Because God knows what might happen if we scare her."

"And if she changes her mind? Or if we're too late? She's got her child back, Arthur. The cops found the animal and got *her* child back."

"They didn't find anyone."

"What?"

Arthur stood and pulled open a drawer. "The cops haven't arrested anyone," he said with his back to Sarah again. "Cara showed up at her front door at four in the morning, dropped off like an orphan abandoned on some church steps." He turned around and slid a piece of paper across the table. It was an article printed from the computer. "She disappeared from her bed, just like May." He tapped the paper with an index finger. "They were in the room next door, just like May." He tapped again. "And they heard a loud bang and crying that wasn't her." He tapped one last time. "*Just like May.*" He gestured with his hands. "Gone into thin air. And returned the same way."

Sarah picked up the paper.

"Let me talk to her first. I'm begging you."

Sarah studied the paper for an excruciatingly long time. "I can't," she said finally, and Arthur dropped his head. "I'm going to the police tomorrow."

He clenched his teeth. "May is *our* daughter, goddammit!" He edged forward, but brought his voice back to normal. "I'm tired of you trying to control this. I've done nothing wrong to you."

"It's what you're doing to yourself."

He backed away. "I'm going to talk to her," he said, his voice full of confidence. "I've been here, in *my* home," he pointed at the floor, "living and breathing this for almost seven months. You upped and left. *You bailed.*"

"That's not fair," Sarah said, her lip curling. She glared at him from under her eyebrows.

"*That's* not fair? Well, son of a bitch!" He looked around the room dramatically, laughing. "You know what's not fair? Slowly killing myself while you self-preserve." He lifted his shirt, displaying his ribs, which were prominent along with his hips, leading down into his waistline. His skin was paler than usual and his extensive tattoos were vibrant, the black script rising and falling over the speed bumps of his ribcage. "You talk about a mother having her heart torn out? What about you, leaving when things get too hard?" He shook his head. "You do what you have to do, Sarah. And I'll do what I have to do."

She stood up, grabbed her coat off the back of the chair, and turned for the door.

"Run away." Arthur called from behind. "You're good at that. Never in a million *fucking* years did I imagine this would be you!"

She pulled open the front door and slammed it shut behind her.

"You don't deserve a child," he yelled.

11:56 PM

The room spun above him. He was flat on his back, arms and legs spread like a star. The bottle of beer in his right hand was a swig from empty, so he sat up, drank it, and threw it full force at the bureau mirror, shattering it into a million tiny pieces. The shards shimmered in the amber glow of the streetlight outside before raining down with a tinkling all over the dresser and hardwood floor. He stood over Sarah's side of the bed, still neatly made and undisturbed, and picked up a fresh bottle of beer from the six-pack carton. He twisted it open and poured the suds all over the blanket. The beer foamed and then absorbed into the fabric, soaking in like a sponge. A growl escaped his throat, and he ripped the blanket from the bed, throwing it to the floor. With a burst of strength, he lifted the mattress and flipped it toward the dresser. It didn't make it completely over, catching on the side and folding momentarily before springing back into place, oblique on the bed platform. Using the back of his hand, he swung to his left and batted the lamp off the nightstand. It crashed into the wall and fell to the floor. He yanked the drawer from the stand and dumped its contents onto the mattress. Lotions and nail polish and cotton balls all spread across the bottom sheet. He shuffled to the walk-in closet and jerked open the door. It banged into the wall and the doorknob left an indentation where it struck. He entered the small room.

Perhaps half of her clothes remained – she hadn't taken all of them in her haste to leave. He pulled everything off the hangers. The clothes, plastic draped over some of them, fell in a heap on the floor. He kicked at the shoes on the rack below, stomping them as they fell over, breaking the high heels. He burst back through the door and into the bedroom where their wedding picture caught his eye. He turned and drove his left fist through the glass and into the wall behind the frame. Shards pierced his skin, pinned between his knuckles and the crushed drywall. He stumbled and dropped to the floor, turning his back to the wall and sitting on top of the now mangled wood and glass. He rested the back of his head on the wall.

Tuesday, October 6, 2015, 6:10 AM

It was morning when a car driving down the road, wet from an overnight rain, provided just enough noise to wake him. The light in the room forced him to squint, and he brought his hand up to shield his eyes. He was met with agony. Glass shards were embedded deep in his skin behind and in between his knuckles. He bent his fingers and shuddered as the skin, swollen and desperately trying to heal, tore further. He clenched his teeth and pulled each piece, one by one, from the flesh. Infection would not be far off if he didn't clean up. Each piece of glass was tinged a different shade of red and, as he dropped each shard on the floor, they resembled a tiny, dissected pane of stained glass. The blood began to flow freely once the obstruction was removed. The searing pain of the wound quickly quelled a brief feeling of relief from the release in pressure. He pushed himself to his feet and pulled open the closet door, leaving a streak of blood across the white paint, and stumbled through into the bathroom. Fussing with the knob until it finally spun, he pushed his bleeding hand under the ice-cold water. It stung like the faucet were spitting razors at his skin. The water ran red, then pink, and finally clear. Meaty walls of skin exposed themselves for a brief moment before they welled with fresh blood.

The tweezers were in the medicine cabinet, and he began prying at the wounds, looking for any remnants of glass. He found two small pieces before dropping the tweezers into the sink, unable to continue poking and prodding. He rinsed it again, trying to eyeball the cuts. Nothing else stood out. He pulled a hand towel from the hook and wrapped it tightly around his hand, applying pressure. To gain leverage, he sat on the toilet seat and slipped the wrapped hand under his thigh. The weight made it throb, but it finally subsided enough for him to take a deep breath.

He rested his back against the tank and slumped against the wall. With his free hand, he pulled his pack of cigarettes from the breast pocket of his shirt. They

---

caught on the flannel and he worked them free, flipped open the box, and grabbed a butt with his lips.

5:35 PM

"Hey, Simon."

"Arthur. How are you?"

"Peachy."

Simon laughed under his breath, barely audible on the other line.

"Anything?"

"Nada."

Arthur stared through his car window at the gray house across the road. Smoke wafted from the cigarette in his bandaged hand. "Figured as much. Thanks."

"Take it easy, bud."

He tossed his phone onto the seat next to him without looking as a breeze whizzed through the car.

The house was mid-sized but impeccably maintained, with a manicured lawn and a bed of flowers bordering the front. It was set back about twenty yards, and the left side of the property cut into a hill which continued to slope down the front lawn, obscuring a portion of the lower level from the road. *Must be fun to sled down*, he thought. *Cara will enjoy it this winter.*

It would likely take Codi about twenty-five minutes to get from her office to her house. Factor in rush hour and 5:45 was realistic, yet at 5:39 a car rolled down the road, turned on its blinker, and pulled into the driveway. The door opened and Codi emerged. Arthur pushed open his own door and propelled himself from the car, flicking his cigarette onto the side of the road in the process. Seeing something move from the corner of her eye, Codi glanced at him, then continued walking to her door. Only after a second did she pause.

"Codi?" he called out in a friendly tone. She backed slowly towards her door, her expression changing to one of uncertainty. Fear, even. Arthur held out his hands in front of him. "No, no, I'm just here to talk to you."

"I'm sorry about what I said to your wife," she said, still moving backwards. "I didn't mean to start any trouble. I was just trying to help." She stumbled over a protruding paver, but caught herself on the stone wall that edged the driveway.

"Hey, I'm just here to talk with you," he said calmly. "Not looking to start to start any trouble."

She placed one high-heeled foot on the bottom step. "How do you know where I live?"

"I have your information at the shop," he said. "I'm sorry I used it and just showed up like this, but I really need to talk to you."

She nodded.

"Did you see my wife at work today?"

"No. She wasn't in. I checked. I wanted to speak with her."

Arthur shook his head. "It's best you didn't. Deal with me right now and just leave her alone. She's not in a good place. She told me what you said to her."

"And you think I'm crazy."

"No," he said.

"Then what?"

"I want to know why you said what you did. I want to know what you know. And I want to know why you know it."

She glanced up at her front door and stood quiet for a time. "Come inside," she said, standing up straight. "I'll make some coffee, and I'll tell you everything I know."

Arthur looked up at the house and back to Codi.

"My parents took Cara shopping. There's no one here besides us. We can sit out back if you'd feel more comfortable."

Arthur nodded. "Okay."

"The only thing is," she started, "you have to let me finish explaining before asking any questions. You can ask me absolutely anything you want after, but I have to tell you it all first."

"I can do that," he agreed.

5:54 PM

The gauze was now stained red in blotches of varying sizes, the biggest directly over the middle knuckle. Codi set down two mugs and sat across the table from Arthur. Steam swirled from the tops. "Is milk and sugar enough? I have cream if you want it."

"This is fine," he said, having no intention of drinking the hot coffee.

"What did you do to your hand?" she asked, alarmed, noticing the bandage for the first time.

"Broke a glass washing it last night. I was spaced out." He fiddled with the spoon next to his mug.

She changed the subject. "I thought for sure your wife would've called the police. I was nerve-racked all day."

"In the spirit of full disclosure, I have no idea what she's doing right now."

She wrinkled her eyebrows.

"The wife and I aren't together presently." Out of habit, he dragged the coffee closer to him. "She left me last month."

"She left you?" There was judgment in her voice.

He nodded. "She tells me I've abandoned her, and I suppose she has a point, considering I've abandoned myself." He had no clue why he was telling her these things, but he continued. "But my daughter has been gone for the last seven months and I'm quite fucking petrified, and so I'm doing everything in my power to get her back. I wasn't the best about it. I've been drinking. Just trying to navigate all of this." He looked up at Codi who had taken a seat and was staring at him from across the table. She sipped her coffee. "Sorry," he said.

"Nothing to apologize for."

"I'm sure I'm preaching to the choir anyway."

"You are. Except I don't have anyone to answer to. And while that sucked, I didn't have to deal with anyone else's feelings." She caressed the handle of the mug. "But it definitely sucked."

Arthur admired the back of the house. It was taller than it was wide and modernly constructed. The backyard was private on all sides but Arthur's left, where the grass stretched to the sidewalk that traced the outline of the subdivision like a ribbon. "If you don't mind me asking, where is Cara's father?"

"Your guess is as good as mine. But I'd imagine he's not working, watching Netflix and smoking weed."

"Sounds like a gentleman."

"You don't know the half." She sipped more coffee. "Don't sleep with people you barely know. And if you do, pull out."

He accepted the wisdom with a smirk. "Was he ever in her life?"

"He was, before my stomach started growing. He was fascinated with the idea of being a father, until he realized that he'd actually have to be a father. When I started to show, when it became real, he started to pull back. I saw it right away, so I prepared myself. He tried to convince me to have an abortion. I was five months pregnant. Then he tried convincing me it wasn't his. I'm not a whore, contrary to how I'm sure I'm coming off right now."

Arthur shook it off.

"He tried anything he could to get out of it. Inevitably, Cara was born, and, after getting home from the hospital, he came to visit, looked at her, asked me how I was doing, asked if I needed anything, and then left. He never held her. Never touched her. Not once. To this day."

"Did you let him go?" Arthur asked, disturbed at the idea that someone wouldn't want to be around their child, no matter life's circumstances.

"I went after him for support, and I was awarded it. But he was broke. He stopped working all together. In and out of jail, you know the story. He came around a few times when Cara was a little older." She paused momentarily. "But it was bullshit. And there wasn't much the state could do, money-wise. I could keep having him sent to jail, but what was that going to do for me?

"Then, out of the blue, he got a job working construction. Made decent money, according to the lawyers. I thought he might've gotten his head out of his ass, but it was all because he'd met a girl. A no bullshit type. He'd wanted to impress her. Probably lied and told her it was his company. They started taking money from his checks, garnishing him, so he couldn't afford much. I know how much I was getting once the checks started to come in – either he was making a lot or they were killing him for what he'd owed." She absentmindedly brushed dirt from the table.

Arthur zipped his sweater a little higher.

"I didn't mean to scare your wife the way I did."

Here we go, Arthur thought.

"I'm still reeling. I'm not *okay*. My daughter is home, and maybe I'll feel okay one day, but that's not the way it works. Arthur, when you find your daughter-"

When.

"-you'll understand."

Where is she going with this?

She stared him in the eyes. "I'm the reason your daughter is missing."

With those words, he figured he'd tense and his blood would boil. He had imagined hearing them from some bastard. A fat man with a beard, handcuffs restraining him. He'd spit in his face. Punch him. Shoot him. Who would put him away? And even if they did, it would be worth it. No, it would not. He would lose years of his daughter's life – even more time than he had already lost.

But if she had been found dead. Or if she hadn't been found at all …

But instead of anger, a draping, cold curtain fell over him. Pins and needles pricked his extremities, his nerve endings firing.

Codi didn't move. She only stared just beneath Arthur's gaze. She stared through him. Waiting, bracing herself for the explosion that never came.

"Please just give me a chance to explain," she said. "I promise that it'll make sense if you do."

He clenched his teeth and nodded slightly.

"Believe me when I tell you it wasn't on purpose. That doesn't make sense right now, but it will." Her posture straightened, and she leaned in. "I need you to listen to me and believe what I say." She blinked and kept her eyes closed a little longer than normal. "None of this is permanent. And you will have your daughter back just the way I have mine."

A wind whipped through the backyard, loosening some dead leaves.

"I'm listening." His face was hard, his jaw muscles tense.

She rubbed her forehead with the tips of her fingers. "Do you remember the bang?"

"Yes."

"Like a bomb. And then the sounds. The squealing, the screaming."

Arthur could hear them whenever he wanted. They were seared into his brain.

"For months, those sounds echoed in my ears," she said. "I pestered the police about them, but they dismissed it. They were more concerned by the lack of evidence at the scene. I could see the look on their faces whenever we sat down to discuss the case. They had nothing. I knew it and they knew it, but they still tried to conceal it."

"Were you ever suspected?" Arthur asked.

"Never. Not after the initial procedure. My parents were home when it happened. And I hadn't been there immediately before she disappeared. I was out with a friend. There just wasn't enough time for me to do anything.

At first, I stayed home all day, waiting for her to come home. Standing at the front door, staring out into the street, hoping a police car would show up with my daughter in the back. If my phone reception was low, I'd panic. It was always charged fully. I didn't go anywhere without knowing I'd have access to my phone. I was a basket case. But throughout all of it, that screaming, the high-pitched cries, they lingered. Haunted me at night. I couldn't sleep. I started imagining things, noises from her bedroom. I could hear her calling my name at night whenever I would start to doze off. They gave me Xanax and other pills I can't pronounce. None of it worked long enough. I felt helpless. So I started to read. I read everything about child abduction I could get my hands on. I spent hours a day at the library and on my computer. The more I read, the more I started to notice a trend in this area. At first, it seemed like there was no rhyme or reason. Some kids were still missing, some were found, but when I studied the ones who'd been found, I noticed a pattern. Not with all of them, there were some anomalies, but I would say a good amount. When one child was found, another went missing on the same day, somewhere else. Because some were discovered in the middle of the night, there was no way to determine exact times, but they all seemed to be damn near to the minute."

A car drove by, the tires gliding across the asphalt.

"And all of them were found in the same places from where they'd disappeared. Their beds most of the time, but there were other places too. Daycares. Supermarkets. Didn't matter how old the kids were, though the vast majority of them were too young to even speak or communicate anything they might've seen."

Arthur shifted in his seat. His leg was asleep, but he ignored it, absorbed in Codi's words. She spoke them with conviction, though she barely looked at him. Instead, she held her cup of coffee and stared into the distance, reliving every moment as she described them.

"Those few who were old enough to relay any information had zero recollection of being gone. They'd simply gone to sleep and woke up in the morning, like nothing had happened. Same with the young boy in the grocery store. Two-and-a-half, in the same aisle, wearing the same clothes. That was in 1985. There isn't a story to go with all of them, and even fewer interviews with the families, but the statistics don't lie."

"What made you relate them all?" Arthur asked. "Cara hadn't shown up at your door yet, right? So what made you identify with these kids?"

"At first?" she asked. "Optimism. All of them had vanished without a trace, like Cara. It wasn't a lot to go on but, as you know, it's easy to grasp at straws when you're desperate." She drank more coffee. "But that wasn't all. I found an article from 1927. A four-year-old child named Richard. Up and vanished from his backyard in Frenchtown, NJ while his mother hung clothes on the line. The mother said the last thing she heard was the yells of a man. She became disoriented for a few seconds and then she heard the bang. Loud. Made her eardrums buzz, she said. They found the kid in his backyard two months later.

"Another article, this one from 1998, somewhere in Bucks County, I can't remember where exactly, a little girl, also four, disappeared out of her bed. Her father was brushing his teeth. They also found her back in that same bed, almost a year later."

"Can you show me these articles?" Arthur asked.

She stood up and opened the back door of the house, pulling a thick binder packed full of paperwork from somewhere inside, then walked back and slid it over to him. "Everything is in there. I printed it all and showed it to the authorities. They ignored most of it. 'We appreciate your help, but we have people on every inch of this stuff,' they told me."

Arthur flipped it open and leafed through the pages. They were in order and color-coded. Lines were highlighted, sticky notes attached all over the place, and certain pages were dog-eared.

He looked them up and down without blinking, stunned. He reached around the book and took his coffee mug by the handle. "This is detailed," he said, taking a sip and returning the mug to the table.

"It was my entire life," she said, sitting down again.

Another gust of wind. This one shook the table.

Arthur turned the page. Articles on top of articles. He stopped as one in particular caught his eye:

Man On Deathbed Claims Missing Son Is Still Alive

CRUX, SUNDAY, OCTOBER 20, 1981 – Richard Porter, 94, died at home early Sunday morning. Porter, a well-known and respected citizen of Crux, was the owner of Crux Furniture, a staple of the town since the early 1950s. A master carpenter, he designed furniture for many high-end clients and for his own retail store. He had suffered through a multitude of ailments in the final years of his life. Strange, however, are the words he allegedly uttered before passing on.

"He said, 'My son is still alive. Please alert the police.' And he was very serious about it. Mr. Porter was not one to kid around," said Mira Verango, his live-in caretaker for the better part of two years.

Porter's son, Daniel, went missing on Halloween in 1932, or forty-nine years ago next week. The younger Porter was on two-week leave from the Navy and was said to have gone missing from his childhood home. He was twenty years old at the time. No suspects have ever been taken into custody.

The Crux police have not said whether or not they will reopen the case, though it is unlikely. Richard Porter was said to have been of sound mind at the time of his death.

Services will be held ...

Arthur stared incredulously at the words. He rubbed his chin. "So what now? What does all of this have to do with my daughter? What do *you* have to do with it?"

"Flip to the last page in the book," said Codi.

Local Man Arrested After Warning Locals of Possible Child Abductions.

CRUX, SUNDAY, JUNE 5, 2012 – John Braun, of Crux, was taken into custody on Saturday after a public disturbance. It was reported he was yelling obscenities at anyone within earshot. When he was not cursing, he was allegedly warning everyone of someone abducting children.

"He was going nuts," a bystander says. "'You'll hear them coming when the screaming starts!' he said. It was crazy. 'It'll take your children. It'll force you to do bad things to other people's children.' He seemed out of his mind."

Braun was said to have been carrying around a liter of vodka and drinking between rants. He was booked and charged with disturbing the peace and public intoxication.

Arthur looked up.

"Read the comments underneath," Sarah urged. "I printed those out too. The first one. Read that."

"John is peaceful, normally," Arthur read aloud. "Never yelling or raving. But he is known for talking about some unusual stuff, and it's not the first time he's brought up children. Almost positive he's homeless, as he's always downtown. Usually a nice man. Doesn't really bother anyone. Better than the other crap that litters the benches. Sad to hear he's on hard times."

"So he's a nutjob."

Codi finished her coffee. "I went to see him."

"You found him?"

"Mmhmm. Have you ever been to Crux?"

"Sure."

"Route 223 runs right through the downtown area. It turns into Broad Street, the main drag. I found him in front an old five and dime store, sitting on a bench, hanging out with his dog." She made a face. "This dirty old bulldog. I could smell it from where I stood. At first, I thought the smell was coming from John, but John didn't really stink. Unless the dog just smelled that much worse."

A truck drove by and she paused. Arthur was antsy now. He'd shifted himself a few times.

"I told John that I'd read about him being arrested, and that something about what he'd said led me to him."

"You'll soon be glad you did, lady," he said to her. He kept playing with his beard. A long, thick, braided beard. She began to tell them about her daughter, but he stopped her immediately. "Let me guess. You've a little one missing. Up and disappeared like money on the sidewalk?"

She asked him how he knew.

"Because everyone comes here to tell me, in one way or another. They always find me. Not hard, really. Look at me!" He held his hands out to the side, displaying himself. "Though I suppose it's a bit rough trusting someone like me, isn't it?"

"He spoke unlike anyone I'd ever heard before," Codi said to Arthur. "Surely nothing I'd expect from a man living on a bench in eastern Pennsylvania. He was *nothing* like the person I'd read about in the newspaper. Not then, anyway. He enamored me. I would've taken him at face value no matter what he said, I think. I didn't understand that then, but it was true."

John Braun took Codi's hand into both of his and caressed it, staring deep into her crystal blue eyes with his own. They were compassionate. He was serious, the lines on his face settling into their natural, comfortable place.

"Your daughter is alive, my dear."

Codi broke down on the sidewalk, sobbing hysterically. "Why would you say that to me?" she asked. "How do you know?"

"Because they're always alive. They never die. They just wait." Braun led her by the hand to a table and chairs set up in front of the store. "Sit. And listen closely to me."

She took a seat at the very edge of one of the chairs, leaning forward, not taking her eyes off him. He sat across from her. The round white table that separated them was made of plastic, a cheap backyard table meant for hotdogs and corn on the cob.

"Sometime in the early days of Crux, amongst an early settlement of folks, the natives and the new locals lived in peace with each other. In the beginning, when life was tough for the newcomers and food was scarce, the natives fed the settlers what they could spare. However, as time went on, families grew comfortable and independent, and, eventually, self-sufficient.

"The natives and the settlers had learned to live in the presence of each other, but that's not to say tensions were never aroused during their day-to-day lives. And not everything is written in the history books.

"The story has it that two native children made friends with some of the children in the settler community. They played frequently together until, one day, a man named Emeric Lawson, a higher up in the group of settlers, decided it wouldn't fly anymore. He was a nasty man. His people were self-sufficient, and he demanded no more association with the red-folk, as he called them, for risk of becoming vulnerable again. The settler children, playful and innocent, ignored the order, and continued to associate with the natives, inviting them into their homes at times. When one of Lawson's own children, a little boy of eight years old, was caught playing with a native child, he was reprimanded so badly that he was said to have lash marks on his arms for weeks. A short time later, Lawson caught two native children sneaking around the grounds. He lured them to his home where he beat them until they expired and buried them in the woods, miles away. Figuring the natives would seek revenge if they found out, Lawson decided to allow them to think the young children had gone missing on their own while trying to sneak over to the settlement. Not only did the normally reserved and peaceful Lenape natives not buy it, knowing Lawson's temperament, they acted quickly in response, kidnapping three of the settlement's young children, including Lawson's son. Lawson's temper flared, and he demanded the return of the children or he would send his men to retrieve them, with the promise of much bloodshed. But the tribe wouldn't budge. They demanded the release of their children first. Lawson denied responsibility outright. Instead, he secretly offered the natives another child from his own community for the release of his son. Offended by the proposal, the natives killed Lawson's boy without hesitation.

"The settler community wanted nothing to do with a violent battle. Instead, after being told of Lawson's horrific proposal, they chose to peacefully negotiate with the tribe. They invited them to their grounds to search where they wished, hoping the natives would see that there were no children being held captive.

"Lawson was furious as, in his sociopathic mind, his community had abandoned him. He decided to try to spark a fire in his people by kidnapping a child from his own settlement in an effort to convince the community that the natives were savages. He snuck into the bedroom of one of his fellow men and managed to take a child without being caught. He bound the child to a tree far out into the woods, where he left the boy to be eaten by animals. He then retreated to his own home, where only his wife, who had been threatened with death if she ever spoke a word, knew of his actions. After the ensuing chaotic search for the young boy, who was found dead three days later, his innards pulled out by some hungry creature, the community was horrified and reeling. The natives swore off any involvement, deeming it disgusting and despicable. They placed blame on Lawson and even freed the two remaining children as a show of good will. Slowly, the community came around on the idea, as well. After careful deliberation, they began to believe what the natives had accused Lawson of.

"Because they had not reacted violently, the way he had hoped they would, and completely oblivious of their suspicion, Lawson decided to strike again. This time, the family was ready. The father, a man named Phineas Crichton, had been sleeping near the front door, weapon in hand. He awoke to Lawson's breaking and entering and pummeled him, knocking Lawson unconscious and nearly killing him. When Lawson came to, he was tied to a pillar, his wife restrained next to him. He begged and pleaded, at first cordially, explaining what his true intentions were – that he was making sure the community was safe and secure. But his people would have none of it, and he soon turned violent, flailing and enraged like an animal. The settlers hanged them both. First the wife, so Lawson could watch, and then Lawson himself."

Codi sat staring at Braun.

"A few weeks went by. The community was very uneasy, with a sense of something amiss. Then, one night, Phineas Crichton exploded from his home, running out into the street, brandishing his rifle. His son was missing from his bedroom. Crichton was calmed and a search party immediately set about combing the grounds for the little boy. Nothing turned up after hours of looking, which stretched until nearly noon. Crichton vehemently blamed the natives, claiming to hear them crying aloud while making away with his child. But, according to his own people, it was impossible. No one would have gotten away so quickly, without so much as making himself known in one way or another. No cries of the child were heard, no footprints found on the soft summer ground.

"Crichton spent his days roaming the grounds and the local woods, cursing the natives and speaking of Lawson's truth. He spent hours a day approaching every single person in the community, searching for some hope. Every day, they would answer with nothing new. As the months went by, Crichton slipped further and further into the depths of despair, ceasing to eat or even sleep. He took sick not long after that and, on his deathbed, in hallucinatory hysterics, screamed to the doctor at the top of his lungs that he wished it were the doctor's child who had been taken away, not his own. Crichton perished within hours. At the same time, after what sounded like a stampede of horses and human hollering, audible to everyone in the immediate area, Crichton's young son was found in his bedroom, no worse for wear. It was the doctor's son, however, who simultaneously went missing from his own bedroom.

"It became a cycle. And the community, which thought itself to be haunted by Lawson's spirit, began to fall apart at the seams. One child after another was abducted in the same manner, only to be returned after the family wished the situation upon someone else. Committed another child to whatever it was stalking them. Sacrificed them.

"No longer trusting of each other, the settlement quickly abandoned the area, part of which would much later become known as Crux." John Braun held out his hands, gesturing to the entire town around him. He caressed his braided beard. The dog looked up at his movement and then settled its head back down on top of its paws.

"You were here with your family before your daughter's disappearance. Here or somewhere close. Vance State Park, I'll bet."

Codi nodded and Braun smiled.

"You must do as Crichton did, then. As everyone else has done since then. You must commit another child. Someone who has been here. It's the only way."

The homeless man sat back in his chair, his fingers clasped across his chest. "You don't think you believe me at this moment, and that's natural. But you'll leave here and you'll realize that you do believe me. You'll believe me because it's the only thing you have. What else have you got to lose? Then you'll hold your child in your arms and won't regret your decision for some time. But you will regret it. That's the evil in this … this curse.

"I've been here a long time," said Braun. "A long, long time. And they all end up here. For good reason."

Arthur's expression was blank. Codi didn't know what to make of it. The temperature had dropped considerably and she shivered. He sat motionless, eyes locked on her, the binder still open in front of him.

"I looked for any record of him once I got home. I found nothing. No proof of a John Braun anywhere in the area. None that matched him, I mean. It's a common name. It blends in. Which is why I believe he made it up. And I know there's more to him than I ever found out. But I didn't care anymore. I just saw my way out of the situation and never looked back. It's selfish. But it's what happened."

"Why May?" he demanded.

She paused, the answer somewhere close but not quite at her lips. "I didn't know she was your daughter," she said, finally. "That doesn't make it right or acceptable, but it's the truth."

"You're right," he said.

"Your wife was invisible. She was a face in the hall. I knew her, but not well. She had been at the outing with us. She was pregnant. I didn't know if it would work. I couldn't remember who else had their children with them that day, and I didn't want to go asking. I felt like everyone knew my intentions. It was stupid, but I was being careful. She was my only hope." Codi looked down. "So I decided to do it and then quit, so I wouldn't have to see the consequence of my decision. It was the coward's way out." She stood up and the chair slid backward. "Hell, I wasn't even sure it was going to work. But I was desperate." She fiddled with her hands and paced a few steps back and forth. "I didn't know how well acquainted I'd need to be. I didn't know anything aside from what he told me, and it all seemed nuts. But, I was willing to try anything. I was on my own and playing a guessing game." She stopped and looked at him. "You have to understand. I know that deep down you do. I'm telling you that you can have your daughter back. It sounds insane and ridiculous, but it's true. My daughter is out buying new clothes right now. Shopping with my parents, like any other kid."

Now Arthur stood and rubbed his temples. "Let's say any of this is true," he blurted out. His chair caught a gap between pavers and wouldn't move any further. He reached behind and fiddled with it until it gave way, allowing him to move from behind the table. "Let's say everything you're telling me is gospel."

She waited for an elaboration, but Arthur said nothing else. He balked at his own words.

"Then how could I go through with it?" she finished for him.

Arthur shrugged.

"He could've told me to murder someone myself ... and I would have."

"Ahhhh." He waved his hand in frustration and turned away.

"And so would you."

"You're so confident of that?" His voice went up a notch as he turned back around. "You don't know me at all. How can you tell me that I'd be perfectly fucking fine taking another child away from their parents?"

"Because I saw the way you spoke about your daughter," she said. "The gleam in your eyes. The gushing coming from every bit of you, even though you tried to keep it subdued for me. You think I didn't battle with myself before doing it? I did what I had to do for my family. We all do what we have to do. It's nature. It's what it is."

He wanted to leave. To run to his car and get the hell out of there. Drive to his wife. Tell her everything. And then what? Tell the police? What the hell would that accomplish? *There's a crazy bitch telling me ghost stories about my kid!* Or, worse yet, if he took Codi at face value. *Officer, some evil cocksucker of a ghost steals kids and encourages people to sacrifice the children of others!* It was asinine. It was demented. And Arthur believed every word of it. He believed it whole-heartedly.

Sarah would have the loony bin come for him, and she would have Codi arrested.

Codi walked closer to him. She sighed deeply. "I stayed because I deserved to see what I had done." She fought the tears for a moment but the emotions exploded out of her. "I heard about your daughter a few days later, after your wife hadn't been at work for a little while. Jesus, even with Cara home, I didn't completely believe that it would happen." She sniffed hard and put her hands up to her face. "Oh, God, when I heard it was true, I wanted to die. I wanted to die. I kept thinking about what a piece of shit I was. How could I willingly put someone through what I had just been through? How is that any better than physically taking someone's child away from them, kicking and screaming? I was the devil. I am the devil. I know that." She began wailing. Her hands trembled at her eyes. "I just couldn't sit back and let you go through it anymore. Every day I look at my daughter and it's tainted. I'm a bad person, but I have to believe that most people would do what I did. I have to believe it, because if I don't tell myself that, I don't know what I'll do."

The wind whipped unforgivingly. The chairs, light and flimsy, rocked, ready to give way and topple backwards. The chill was biting. Codi stood before him, mascara running down her cheeks, arms wrapped around herself. "I'm so sorry for what I've done, Arthur. *I'm sorry*. And it's not fair for me to say that if I knew it was you all along, I wouldn't have done it. Because that trivializes it. But it's true." She shivered again, her teeth beginning to chatter.

He lifted his arms slowly, starting to reach out to her. Eyes closed, oblivious to the advance, Codi continued hugging her own body. He took a step forward and the wind whipped again. Her hair danced wildly in the air.

He dropped his arms and stepped back. The cold was bothering him now too, permeating through the thick knap of his hooded sweatshirt. He jammed his hands in his jean pockets, confused with himself.

"Do you want to come inside?" she asked, her eyes now open. She had settled down a bit, the hysterics calming. He looked at her and could not help but feel bad. She had just lain herself bare to someone she barely knew, with the most incredible and ridiculous story. To someone who, for all she knew, might have reacted differently. Angrily. Violently. A single mother who had just been through hell, the same hell he was going through now. Her fault or not, intentionally or not, she took a risk by doing what she did. He could see that.

"If you, you know, have any questions or anything. Or just want to talk about it. Or vent. I don't know. I understand if you don't want to or don't feel comfortable. Or if you want to leave and never speak to me again. Whatever it is you want to do."

Arthur looked around. What was left? A cancerous marriage. The loneliness in the lack of answers. A drink. A smoke. Nothing.

"I'll come in," he said.

5.

Wednesday, October 7, 2015, 4:00 PM

Arthur removed his phone from the dashboard receptacle and unplugged it. He popped a bunch of quarters into the meter, giving him a few hours. For the third day in a row he looked up and down the block for the man named John Braun. No one even vaguely matched Codi's description. He would, once again, have to roam the town hoping to find a needle in a haystack. It had been some time since Codi met Braun. There was no telling whether or not the man was even alive, never mind in the same town, with the same look, standing in front of the same store. But Arthur needed to start somewhere.

He stretched himself out after the better part of an hour in the car. The day was typical of early October. Breezy and chilly, but when the sun was unobstructed, it was warm enough. The leaves had begun dripping off the trees like coffee from a cone, faster with each passing day. There was no place in the world like the Northeast in the fall. It starts in late August, when the air is still hot and only the keenest of senses can feel the change. Then September comes along and, no matter how temperate and warm the weather may seem, the cooler nights sneak in quietly and quickly, as if waiting to strike. By the end of the month, the fragile deciduous trees begin throwing off their leaves one by one. The entire month of October is a sight. Greens start to yellow further and reds and oranges take over, providing a palette rich enough for an artist to paint with.

People come from all over the world to see this, he thought, looking around him. He had been back and forth, not yet *fully* convinced that any of the story was true, but at the same time, it could all happen in front of his eyes and he was still not sure he would believe it.

He stood next to his car, in front of a house that had obviously been converted into a business. It was cream-colored with two sets of steps leading up to a front porch. The house, obviously very old, looked like it had been wedged between two commercial brick buildings. Like it had stumbled into the wrong area of town and decided to set up shop. But that was the opposite of the truth, as it had been around long before anything else in the vicinity. A relic that at one time tried to blend in with modern Main Street, USA, but now looked aged and antique, especially and ironically in contrast with the modern street lamps and facades of new buildings, constructed and decorated to look older than they were.

"Left or right?" he said aloud. "Where are you, John? Help me out a bit here." He turned to his left and walked across Front Street, over the train tracks, and through the old town. The easterly wind blew against his back, pushing his hair in front of his eyes. He pushed it back. After a mile of fruitless searching, he turned down a side block, came up another, and started back east toward where he had come from originally. Now the wind was at his front, chilling his cheeks and making them red. No sign of Braun yet, but he pressed on, passing even more old-timey buildings and peering down side blocks and into storefronts. A used book store. An Italian ice shop. Restaurants. Eventually, the buildings gave way to almost all residential homes. He pressed on, half looking for the man he hoped to talk to, half dazed and confused, wondering whether he should find the closest psych ward.

It can't hurt to blow off some steam, he thought, and admired the houses that seemed too close to the road. The town was different, but he was used to different now. Different felt comfortable.

Street after street, house after house. Yellow curb, red curb, plain curb. This person needs to cut their lawn. That person takes care of their porch. The cobblestone sidewalk looks better than the smooth concrete, but it sure is harder to push a stroller. Every other block or so was a house turned into a business, primarily doctor's offices or churches, sometimes a convenience store. It felt like another time, and Arthur wondered if he would be able to have a cavity filled by the town notary.

Just as he was ready to turn back, the road opened to another row of businesses, and that's when he saw him. Standing alongside a blue, bi-level restaurant, was a man with long hair pulled back into a bun and a beard down to his chest, held in place by a braid. He wore a cargo jacket, jeans, and the same Chuck Taylors Codi had described. The dog clamored about his feet, licking something up off the pavement. *She was right. That's a heinous beast,* Arthur thought. But a dog, nonetheless, and he longed to pet the dopey bastard.

He felt as if John Braun, who looked precisely how Arthur had pictured him, was a ghost. An apparition of something he had perceived, though non-existent after his search of the last few days. He closed the gap between the two by jogging across the street, even though the right of way was not his. A horn blew to remind him of that. He waved a hand at the bothered car.

"John?" he asked from the corner, about twenty-five feet away from the man and his dog. "John Braun?"

The man turned to Arthur, now merely feet away. He spun back around and began to walk in the opposite direction.

"John, my name is Arthur."

The man continued forward, picking up speed while the dog trailed at his heels, nearly too fat to keep pace.

"I know it's you, John. I have to ask you some things. Please. I've been looking for you for days now."

"I'm not John," the man said. "I don't know anything."

Arthur continued his pursuit. "I don't believe you. I know your name is John."

There was no response other than the padding of John's sneakers as he tried his best to pull away.

"Goddammit, John. Why are you doing this?"

"Leave me alone, you hear? I'm tired of it. I don't need the harassment."

"I'm not here to harass you." Arthur began to jog. "I need your help."

"It's not enough to call me crazy. It's not enough to stare, but you have to record me on your phones now? That's not nice."

"John, my daughter is missing, and I know you can help me." Arthur caught up to him.

After a double take, Braun looked Arthur from top to bottom and back up again, studying his face.

"My name is Arthur."

"I heard you the first time, Arthur. What paper did you read that in? Huh? This another joke?"

Arthur shook his head. "No sir. Not a joke." He held up his cell phone, showing Braun the background image. "Not a joke at all."

"Who …" He seemed puzzled. "Who sent you? Did anyone send you? Or did you stumble here like the others."

"Codi Garret. She told me where to find you."

"That the redhead?" Braun asked.

Arthur nodded.

"Yeah, she was here a few months ago. Closer to a year, I guess." The dog croaked at another dog across the street. It sounded like a longtime smoker with a chest cold. Braun tugged on the leash, and the animal sank down at his sneakers.

"Look, John, I could really use some help right about now. Can I pick your brain? Can we just find somewhere to sit and talk?"

Braun licked his lips and ran his hand along his braid. "Sure. Welcome to my office."

Arthur laughed. "You hungry? How about some dinner?"

"Let me show you my dining room while we're doing the grand tour."

Arthur insisted.

"No can do. These places don't let me in anymore. Not since I was arrested. Not even really before, but definitely not after that charade." Braun's breath was stale, though not sour like someone's might be having gone a period without brushing their teeth. And it didn't smell of alcohol.

"How's this place back here?" Arthur asked. The dog sniffed at his sneakers.

"Seems to be pretty good from the way I hear

people speak of it."

Arthur took off his sweatshirt and held it out to the man. "Toss your jacket behind the building over there and put this on. We'll get it when we come back out."

"What if someone takes it?"

Arthur stared at the holey, weather-beaten jacket. "Then we'll get you a new one," he said. "Come on. Let's eat. I'm starving."

Braun tied the dog to a parking meter a few paces from the door of the building. It sat and stared up at the both of them. Arthur patted its head and it licked his hand.

"Delilah likes you," said Braun.

"How old is she?"

"Five."

Arthur looked over at Braun questioningly.

"She's just sloppy. Her guts are perfectly fine."

"Sounds like my car."

The host stared Braun up and down as they pushed through the front door. "Table for two, please," Arthur said. She hesitated. "Table for two please," he repeated.

She reached for two menus without removing her eyes from either of them. Arthur stared back. "Is there a problem?"

"No. No problem," she said. "Follow me." She led them through the dining room, which was empty at the off-peak hour, and put them at a table in the back corner. "Your waitress will be with you shortly," she said. Arthur thanked her dryly.

The room was comfortably warm. It had a charm about it, restored and taken care of, but had certainly been there a long time. The walls were stone in various sizes and the ceiling was tin with dark wooden beams stretching the length. The floors had not had much work done to them, perhaps a refinishing or two, but it showed the stress of the years. What looked to be the original fireplace took up the center of the far wall and huge windows drowned the room in light, despite its dark interior.

"This has got to be a hundred-fifty years old," said Arthur.

"Two-fifty," said Braun, still looking around uncomfortably. "It was built in the mid-1700s."

"As an inn, I suspect?"

"As a tavern, first. Well, it's always been a bar, but the upstairs was fixed into a hotel sometime in the early 1800s. Once they ran the trains through, it gained popularity." Braun settled into his chair, finally relaxing. "Feels like that long since the last time I was in here." He laughed.

"Are you from here?"

"Earth? Yes. Crux? No. No, I was born in Galloway, New Jersey."

"Moved here as a child?"

"Something like that. My father lost his job, so he upped and moved out here. There weren't many people, but the work was abundant, likely because of that!" He smacked his lips. "Skilled labor was readily available, and he was a master carpenter. He was a skilled man."

"Is he still around?"

"No, he's long passed."

"Sorry to hear that."

"Quite all right," he spun the menu on the table with a dry and cracked hand, his fingernails caked with dirt. "You don't need to do this for me. I'll tell you what you need to know."

Arthur looked up from his menu. "I think I'm going for the BLT. What about you?"

Braun scanned the menu.

"I'm not buying you food so you'll talk. I'm buying you food because it's chilly out and it's almost dinnertime. And there are about twelve things I could choose, so if you don't hurry and pick one I'm going to end up changing my mind to something I don't want."

Braun smiled hesitantly. He wasn't used to handouts – not since his outburst in the town those few years ago. Folks tended to cross the street rather than acknowledge him. And the tourists and outsiders never gave him the light of day, but why should they? He was a filthy bum with a filthy bum dog and a filthy bum life. He had not lived in any legitimate (according the US government) dwelling in more than half a decade. And even when he did, he spent most of his time outside, roaming the town, rain or shine, heat or snow. At least he could hold a job then. Any job. Moving boxes, painting houses, roofing. But his knees were shot, his back was a mess, and he was no longer able to do hard labor. And without proper healthcare, getting treated was impossible, leaving him without work, without money, and without much else. Aside from Delilah.

"You a burger guy?" asked Arthur. His attention was drawn to the front of the room where the waitress and, presumably, the manager on duty were covertly keeping an eye on them. "The Heater looks good," he said, keeping his eyes locked on the pair of them.

"Ignore them," said Braun. "I'm used to it. I'm surprised I'm allowed in here at all. I'd like to go wash my hands, but I'm afraid they'll wonder what I'm up to."

Arthur stood from his chair.

"Don't," Braun said again. "It's okay. Let them stare." Arthur ignored him and started toward the two. They broke their gaze the moment they noticed him. "I was just wondering if we were going to get any service," he asked as he approached.

"Are you ready to order, sir?" the waitress asked.

"You haven't asked us if we want something to drink. You haven't even approached the table. Do you think my homeless friend over there is going to make a scene? Hurt someone? Or does he just not fit in here?"

"No, not at all, sir," the lady said. She was young, likely a college student, and flustered. "I was just looking to see if you were ready for me."

Arthur smiled. "I'm a writer for the Philadelphia Inquirer. I'm in town for a story, but I have no issues writing an aside about a nice little shithole I stopped in for an early dinner on my way through this dirt bag of a town."

The manager overheard the exchange and returned. "Listen, sir-"

"Don't 'listen sir' me," Arthur interrupted. He moved closer to the man, keeping just enough distance between them for personal space. "My buddy John and I are going to have a fantastic dinner. We're going to eat, talk, pay our bill, and get the fuck out of here. Either you want our business or you don't. Either way is fine, but have the decency to tell us. Don't sit back here and stare like the man is some sort of zoo animal. Now serve us some fucking food or tell us to get out."

No one said a word.

"Yes? No?"

"Not at all, sir. We're sorry if we implied anything."

"Good," he said. "We'll have two Yuenglings, please. Also, where's the bathroom?"

Braun was flabbergasted when Arthur returned. "I don't drink anymore," he said, bursting out in a loud cackle, which grumbled into rasp.

Arthur smiled. "Then they're both for me."

The waitress brought the drinks just as Braun returned. "I'll have the BLT, please," Arthur said, pursing his lips after and handing over the hefty menu. She looked over at Braun. "I'll have the fish and chips, please." He too handed over the menu.

"It'll be out in a little while," said the waitress, who returned to the kitchen as fast as she'd come out.

"Can I call you John?"

"Only if you really want to," John replied.

Arthur took a long drink of beer. "Codi and I spoke at length a few days back. She gave me the scoop, which, and I'm sure you'll understand, I'm a bit …" He couldn't find the word.

"Disconcerted."

"And shaken. And unsettled. The insane legend of the kidnapping ghost probably does that to most people, I assume."

"You'd be surprised how believing people can be when their family is threatened."

"My entire life inside of the last six or seven months has been clown shoes. I get it. Between the screams and the bang, the police and their odd way of navigating everything, my wife leaving me," he was counting on his fingers, "and whatever other boomerangs were thrown in my direction, it's fitting."

"Not to mention those." He pointed to the two beers on the table.

Arthur looked down at the glasses. "Tell me, John, is this how it goes? Do I just wish this shit on someone else's kid and I walk away scot-free. A beautiful reunion of father and daughter? My wife comes back to me and I forget everything she's done in the last two months? Is this the Amityville House?

The farther I get, the better everything is?"

"As your friend Codi did. Were you her sacrifice?"

"Apparently. It was an accident."

"It's never an accident," John said. "By nature, it can't be an accident."

By nature.

"It can be if she didn't know I was the husband on the other end."

John stopped.

"We knew each other briefly. I tattooed her."

"You're an artist?" John asked.

"I am. I own a tattoo studio in New Hope."

John freed his arm from Arthur's loaner sweatshirt and then pushed up the sleeve of his own t-shirt. Brandished on his surprisingly muscular arm, in extremely faded black ink which had since taken on a green hue, was an anchor with what appeared to be a rope wrapped around it. It was hard to tell.

"Wow. A buddy do that for you?" asked Arthur.

"A fellow sailor. Not much left to it now, but the memories are there all the same."

Arthur couldn't put a finger on John. His demeanor was not that of someone who had given up on life. Instead, he seemed to have a few things figured out. Maybe even more than Arthur.

"When someone is left without much of a choice, they'll do heinous things," John said. "And when your *choice* is saving the life of your child as opposed to simply letting her go ... well, is that really much of a choice?" He fiddled with a packet of sugar. "Regardless of how someone needs to get there mentally, to be able to go through with it, doesn't matter. The choice is a fairly simple one." He replaced his arm in the sweatshirt. "Maybe forgiving Codi seems impossible, but I can assure you her choice was not a fair one. And you're in her shoes. Will you let things run their course for the sake of morality? On the impossibility that the police will come across your daughter alive and well? Because it won't happen. If you don't do it, she is gone forever."

A wave of nausea crashed in the pit of Arthur's stomach.

"Arthur, did Codi tell you how her child went missing?"

"No."

"The child's father, almost never present in either of their lives, decided, for whatever reason – likely to avoid Codi reporting him to the police for his missed child support payments – to attend work function of Codi's` at Vance State Park. Someone lurking around the grounds approached him, she remembered later. This person, she later assumed, correctly, was another parent going through the same thing you are. He found me, as they all do, and I gave him the story. He'd begun preying on parents in the area, wanting to get to know some of them so he could make his move. It's not hard to spot a father who's uninterested. And for the man, it was his way of avoiding the guilt of destroying someone else's life.

Or trying to avoid it. So he struck up a conversation and found out that Codi's child's father was up shit's creek. He'd gotten a new job, Codi explained, and they were gouging his paycheck something terrible. He wanted a way out. The man gave it to him."

Arthur returned his beer to the table. "Cara's father was involved?"

John nodded. "I presume she never saw him again after that day."

Arthur couldn't comprehend it. Were there people in the world who were that innately lazy and disgusting? People who would rather continue living a life of indolence rather than take care of the responsibilities they had created themselves?

Vile.

Crude.

"And he was never questioned?"

"You're asking the wrong person about that," John said. "But the police can never hold anyone. There's no evidence. No proof of anything. He might've been as guilty as a rat, but it wouldn't matter."

The condensation dripped from the beer bottle as Arthur peeled at the wet label.

"Do you see where I'm coming from?" asked John. "You know just as well as anyone else how cruel life can be, but I'm quite certain that before your daughter up and vanished from her bed, you sympathized with someone like Codi in the same way a civilian sympathizes with a solider blown apart on the battlefield. The good intentions are there, but it's impossible to put yourself in those shoes without experiencing it yourself. There's nothing wrong with that. It's life. Picturing it can only go so far, you see?"

"So now I go ahead and pass it forward. Ignore someone else's pain to make mine go away."

"That's your decision to make," said John. "Committing another child is heinous. But does heinous reign over necessary?"

"Necessary only to me." Arthur said.

"Is there really any other kind?"

After a short time, the waitress returned with their order. Without asking if they needed anything else, she turned and walked away.

"Glad the salt is on the table," John joked. He had not taken his eyes from the battered cod in front of him, complete with potato wedges and malt vinegar.

"Enjoy," said Arthur, watching John lick his chops. "It looks good."

John pushed a piece of fish into his mouth and closed his eyes. At that point, anything would have been exquisite.

Arthur shoved in a bite of sandwich and washed it down with the remains of the first beer. "Let me ask you something else."

"Shoot."

"From the way Codi explained things to me when retelling your story, my situation isn't always an isolated incident. But the accounts are so limited. And it's not just one pipeline, so it seems. We're not the only branch."

"Right."

"So, then, what happened to the other branches? How are we narrowed down to just this one? To just mine?"

John finished chewing. "Who says we are?"

"Are there more?"

"Yes." He shrugged. His braid bounced against his chest. "We don't get to read or see everything. Odd things happen every day. And surely you read and see much more than I do. I haven't had a phone in four years. Who am I going to call?"

"Codi did her homework. She's got a binder the size of an encyclopedia."

"They still make those?"

"Binders?"

"Encyclopedias."

"Not many." Arthur drank from the second bottle. "In all of her research, she didn't find much outside of this area."

"Doesn't mean much."

"I suppose not," said Arthur.

John put the finishing touches on his fish, leaving only the chips. "You were on to something earlier."

"How so?"

"It's long been considered that the only way to end the cycle is to sacrifice your own child. To let them die." He shook his head. "It's all hearsay, but there were and are times that there are less cases than at other times. From what I've seen and from the records."

"Records?" Arthur asked.

"You're not the first to research. You won't be the last."

The hostess led a man and woman into the dining room and sat them on the opposite side. John's voice dropped.

"I had journals full of literature. Used to spend days at the library. If you know it, I've read it."

"Where is all of that now?"

John poured the vinegar all over his potatoes. "I burned them when I began losing my mind. Obsessing over anything will kill you, and I began doing just that. And I drank myself into oblivion." He looked at the bottle at Arthur's lips. "You drink a lot, too."

"Not before this."

"Doesn't taste very good, does it? It's a compulsion, though."

John's words cut through Arthur. "I hate it. How did you know that?"

"This thing drives people to be everything they're not. Take a look at your life. Step back and evaluate it. Evaluate how different you are. It eats you alive."

Arthur sighed. "This is insane."

"Put yourself in my shoes," said John. "A nut bag with a laundry list of crazy stories. Crazy, but true. And now I'm sitting here with a perfectly reasonable person, and I can have an open conversation about something I've been forced to repress most of my life, aside from when desperate parents such as yourself seek me out. Even then, it's not easy to let loose in front of someone who looks like me."

"Why you?"

"Because I'm in the club!" He raised his hand.

"Was it your child?"

John smiled. "It was me."

The man at the table across the room raised his voice at the punch line of whatever joke he was telling. His date laughed loudly in an obviously feigned cackle.

"Well, shit," said Arthur. "When you were a baby?"

"When I was younger." He shrugged. "I guess I attract it, like moths to a flame. Everyone ends up here in Crux, at the hub of it all. Even I ended up here. Not a coincidence. And I can't leave, no matter what I do." He held up his water glass. "Cheers. To Crux. To this restaurant. To home."

"And do you give the same advice to everyone?"

"It depends."

"On what?" Arthur asked.

"On whether or not I think the person can handle it. Whether or not I have any faith at all that using more words than I need to is worth it."

"And me?"

John ate a potato. "I haven't sat down in a restaurant in a long time," he said with his mouth full. "I haven't been spoken to with so much as a modicum of the respect you've shown me in a long time either. I don't know what you came to hear. If it was the bare minimum, then you know all you need to know. Commit someone else and it all goes away. For you."

"And if I want to know more?"

"More than I've already told you?" John asked. "I can tell you all the anecdotes you want to hear."

"So then tell me."

Dinner music started on the sound system, low at first and then a bit louder until whoever controlled it found the desired level. Another three people were seated at the far end. The hostess and waitress were staring at John and Arthur again.

"Let's finish this outside," said John. Before Arthur could answer, John nodded in encouragement. "Let's just go." Arthur signaled for the check. He paid the bill and, after some deliberation, left a 20% tip.

Once outside, John untied Delilah, who'd been patiently waiting. He began taking off the sweatshirt.

"Keep it," said Arthur, patting the dog on her side.

"I shower at the shelter," said John.

Arthur shook his head. "I don't care about that. Just keep it," he urged. "It's getting cold."

John looked down at the thickly lined zip-up. "Thank you, Arthur."

"It's nothing."

They walked around back where John collected his unbothered jacket. He pulled it on over his new sweatshirt.

"The hub of it all, huh?" Arthur said, looking around.

"Where the shit hit the fan. This whole gosh darn area is cursed, Arthur." John said. "Once you step foot anywhere around here, it knows you."

"I don't understand."

"You can't just walk into any supermarket and point out a child. That's not how it works. The land needs to touch the child. Taste them. Learn about them. Then it can come for them." Braun frowned. "Do you know where Vance State Park is, right there outside of town?"

"Used to go to Vance all the time," Arthur said, stuffing his hands in his pockets. "My uncle took us fishing over there."

"Of course you did." John huffed. "If you take 223 out of here, make a left onto Mountain View Drive, a few miles down. Make another left onto Sterner Mill Road and then a quick right onto Richlandtown Road. You'll pass Clymer Road. Keep going. About another mile or two beyond that, you'll notice a clearing through the trees, on the left side. It's right before the road banks hard to the right. You'll know it once you see it. Walk through a ways until you get to another clearing. Maybe 200 yards. There will be a small, rundown house on the property. I believe there are some more answers there."

"What's in there?"

John shrugged. "I don't know. I've never been able to get into the house. It's all private property, government owned or otherwise. Be careful if you decide to go." He turned to walk away but spun back. It confused Delilah. "Nice to meet you, Arthur." He stuck out a hand.

"Pleasure was mine, John." He grabbed John's outstretched hand. "Maybe I'll see you again."

John gave his hand a squeeze. "I hope so."

Wednesday, October 7, 2015, 6:04 PM

The sun dipped in the sky. It was still light but not for much longer. Arthur was parked on the side of Richlandtown Road, staring at what he thought was the clearing. It was hard to tell considering most of the leaves were beginning to the thin, but the road ahead banked hard to the right. There was no shoulder, so he wedged his car in the weeds and dirt. He cut the ignition and immediately turned it back on. Just in case. There was a ringing in his right ear, and he tugged on the lobe.

"What am I doing?" he asked aloud. *You've gone this far down the crazy path*, he thought. *What can it hurt to go a little farther?* He crossed the road and entered through the thicket, zigzagging around the first few trees. The ringing seemed to worsen and all sound had become slightly muffled. He stuck his pinky finger inside his ear and wiggled it back and forth, hoping to stir whatever gunk might have been causing it.

The trees pinched tighter as he made his way through, and their gradient of leaves still blanketed the wood, shunning the sunlight. The ringing in his ear intensified with every step. It was loud and disorienting and threw his equilibrium, making him shake his head back and forth. He leaned on a tree to steady himself and recognized that the brush had already swallowed the car and road.

That's when he heard the voice.

"*Dada.*"

It was small and meek. Or was it the ringing? Probably the ringing. He looked around and again jammed a finger in his ear canal and moved it around. "Hello?" he yelled.

Nothing.

The sun was setting fast, and whatever light was allowed in through the gaps in the leaves was dwindling. Arthur stared into the distance where the clearing should have been. He was, by his estimate, barely a quarter of the way through. His eardrum felt ready to burst. *I'll come back*, he decided, and turned for the car, cupping his hand over his ear and jogging as fast as his disrupted sense of balance could handle. The blue paint of his sedan materialized through the leaves and, after a few feet, the squeal in his head seemed to lessen. Nearly out, it subsided greatly. By the time he made it back to the road, it had all but disappeared.

He climbed into the car and, still rubbing his ear, tried to shift into drive. It wouldn't budge. The car was off.

6.

Wednesday, October 7, 2015, 9:45 PM

"She was wrong, Sarah."

"What do you mean?"

"I went to see her." He moved the phone to his other ear.

"At her house?"

"Yes. At her house." He sipped from his bottle of water, then capped it and dropped it on the end table. "And thank you for not calling the police. I appreciate it." It sounded sarcastic. "She's just having a rough time with her own situation and has a weird way of showing it, that's all."

There was silence on the other line. Convincing Sarah to let it go would be hard, but navigating the newfound circumstances would be even harder if he wasn't able to get her off his back. It was the only way to buy enough time to figure out his next move.

"As soon as I pulled up she broke down crying

and apologized immediately. She said she's been going through some really serious issues and said she feels like everything is her fault, because of the lack of answers with her case and how closely related the two situations are. She thinks that had she been able to guide the police better and see who returned her daughter to her, that she would've been able to prevent our situation from happening. So, she feels guilty." He had rehearsed what he was going to say before calling, but it sounded robotic, so he went off-script. "It's like survivor's guilt, you know? She feels bad because she's got her daughter back and we don't have ours. She feels responsible in some weird, twisted way. She's seeing a shrink about it. Just stay away from her. And she'll stay away from you. Pretend it never happened. Ignore it, and so will I. We'll get back to what's important." Nervous that he'd begun to ramble, he stopped and listened.

"Fine."

He knew that tone. She used it when she thought she was right but did not want to continue with an argument. He hoped that would be the case.

"But Arthur, if she even comes near me, I'll call the cops on her right then and there."

Success. "Good," he said, trying hard to hide his contentment. "One less thing for us to worry about."

For him to worry about.

Thursday, October 8, 2015, 10:22 PM

"Wutcha drinking?"

Arthur spun around on his bar stool. "Simon." He shifted his beer to his left hand and shook Simon's hand. "Dogfish Head. Just getting off duty?"

"As always. No bar fights tonight?"

"No dickheads tonight," Arthur said.

"Fair enough." Simon looked at the man sitting next to Arthur.

"This is Mason," Arthur introduced, patting Mason on the shoulder. "He's an artist at the shop."

Simon shook his hand. "Been working?" he asked Arthur.

"Here and there. Stress reliever, you know? Gives me time to think."

"Sure," Simon agreed. "I have to find one of those. Other than the range." He looked to the back of the room. "I'm gonna grab a table. You're both welcome to join me if you want."

"I'm heading out, actually," Mason said, standing and zipping up his sweatshirt. The weight from the metal plugs in his ears swung his lobes back and forth as he moved.

"I'll take you up on it," Arthur said. He patted Mason on the shoulder as he left.

They settled at a four top in the back corner.

"I think I finally know what tattoo I want," Simon said. "A tribal band around my biceps."

Arthur looked up from his beer just in time to catch the smirk on Simon's face.

"How many of those do you get a day?"

"Rarely," Arthur answered. "They went out the window about a decade ago. I'll get some true tribal work sometimes, which is actually a lot of fun. Have you really been thinking about getting one?"

"Not seriously. I would love to, but I'd get tired of anything after a few years. Too indecisive."

"Nothing wrong with that." Arthur raised his sleeve to his shoulder, revealing the completely tattooed upper-half of his arm. "Better than ending up with kanji." He pointed to an area in the center.

Simon laughed. "Let me guess. Eternity?"

"Truth, ironically. Searching for it every day and yet here it is, branded on my arm."

The bartender, Fredo, approached the table.

"You'll get the truth," Simon said after ordering. "Somehow."

Arthur mulled over the statement. "There have been odd cases before, haven't there? Kids missing, disappearing?"

Simon drank some of his beer. "Not since I've been with the department."

"Not in New Hope. But in the area. I'm sure you've heard about them."

"I've overheard the sergeant talking about a few cases like yours," he admitted, seemingly forcing it out. "Very few."

"And most came home, didn't they?"

Simon stared at Arthur. "Yeah," he said hesitantly. The professional in him held back.

"And that's why the department keeps the case so active. That's why we've not been told to expect the worst."

Simon scratched nervously at his forearm. The veins bulged. "I don't know much about any of that. But I do know they're staying as optimistic as possible. Yeah." He grimaced.

Arthur looked down. "I get it. What else are they supposed to say? It's not like they can explain it any better than we can."

"What do you mean?"

"Something's up. Something strange and fucked up. But I'm working on getting to the bottom of it."

"Arthur, let us-"

"Take care of it," he interrupted. "Yeah, I know. I've been hearing it for seven months. And I *do* have faith in the process, but it's not quick enough, and I've been doing some homework." He gauged Simon's reaction. He couldn't afford to blow it by spilling his guts to a cop, as much of a friend as Simon had become. After all he'd just gone through trying to keep Sarah's mouth shut.

"My daughter is alive." He fiddled with a coaster. "Don't ask me why or how I know, because I couldn't answer you even if you did, but she is."

"Your ear is bleeding."

"Huh?" Arthur looked up.

"Your ear," said Simon, grabbing at a bar napkin.

"It's dripping blood."

Arthur reached up and felt the warm trickle just as it beaded to his neck. He took the drink napkin from Simon and sopped up whatever had made its way out, then searched the orifice for any cuts, but to no avail.

"You okay?"

"Yeah. That's never happened before."

"Let's go get it checked out," Simon said. "I'll take you over to the hospital."

"No. No, I'm okay," said Arthur. He stood up. "I'm just gonna go the bathroom and-" He toppled over sideways, pulling the chair down with him. His forehead careened off the corner of a table, and he was unconscious before hitting the floor. After a moment or two, he came to. His vision was blurry and distant and sounds were muffled.

"Help me get him to the car," he heard Simon say, somewhere far away.

11:33 PM

"You have a perforated eardrum," said the doctor. "Blood pressure is slightly elevated. Blood alcohol level is *definitely* elevated. Any sudden, loud noises? Were you standing next to a speaker? Headphones on too loud?"

Arthur shook his head. He thought to mention the ringing in the forest, but withheld.

"Have you flown recently? Changes in pressure?"

"No."

"Cleaning your ears too deeply?"

"Nope."

"Would he typically lose consciousness from a perforated eardrum?" Simon asked from a chair next to the emergency room bed.

"No," the doctor said. "But it's possible your equilibrium went wonky and caused you to fall. You gave your forehead a nice shot. That alone might have done the trick."

"He was out on his feet," Simon said.

"Possible, but highly doubtful given the symptoms. Have you ever stood up too fast and had the blood rush to your head?" the doctor asked.

Simon nodded.

"Think of that times ten. It's blinding, sometimes. I would suggest keeping you overnight to make sure everything is all right, but I really don't think it's necessary. Hang out for an hour, ice your forehead, and we'll check you again. If all is good, you can go home. Sleep it off."

"I'm telling you, I watched his face," said Simon. "I watched him go blank and conk out. He didn't protect himself or anything. Even if you get lightheaded, you're still able to move your arms. He was out."

Arthur spoke up. "I'm okay. I'm not even woozy." He shook his head back and forth to make sure. His brain felt fine, but the knot on his forehead throbbed. He reached up and caressed the protruding lump, about the size of golf ball. It was tender and filled with fluid.

"Anytime anyone loses consciousness, you worry about a concussion. There is the slight possibility that you did, in fact, become unconscious while upright, but I truly don't believe that you were out cold. However, I do believe you," he gestured to Simon with an open hand, "and I'm treating you accordingly. Go home, sleep, take some Advil, and follow up with your primary care physician tomorrow. If you feel the need, we are always here, but I don't think you're going to have any further issues. The perforation is small and right in the center. Keep it dry – use a shower cap in the shower, and no headphones or loud noises, if possible. It will heal on its own. Your doctor will be able to watch it and make sure there is no infection. Again, ibuprofen or acetaminophen if there's pain."

"Would I have heard a ringing because of it?" He felt the lump on his face again. He had a hard time keeping his hands off it.

"Absolutely," said the doctor. "Tinnitus is very common and likely came after it ruptured. Eardrums are resilient. It'll be good as new in no time." He shook Arthur's right hand and noticed the bandage on his left. "What happened here?"

"Broke a glass in my sink."

"Mind if I take a look?"

Arthur unwound the bandage carefully.

"Yikes," said the doctor. "These could've used

some stitches."

"I'm sure," Arthur said. "I just cleaned them well and kept the hand covered."

"You're a mess."

Arthur acknowledged the sentiment.

"Keep it clean and bandaged. Use an antibacterial ointment for a while. I'll have the nurse give you some samples. Take care of yourself, huh?"

"Thanks."

The doctor left the room, and Arthur looked up from under his eyebrows. "I can see it."

"Doc should've drawn an X over it." Simon drew an X in the air.

"Thanks for bringing me," Arthur said. "I appreciate it."

"You covered?"

Arthur nodded. "Took out a policy when the kid was born." His phone vibrated in his pocket. It was a text message from Codi.

"Did you go see our friend?"

"*I did,*" Arthur wrote back. "*And I ended up with a ruptured eardrum, and now I'm in the hospital after slamming my face on a table.*"

"Wife?"

"Huh?" Arthur looked up at Simon. "Oh, no. A friend." The person responsible for his missing daughter. Sure. A friend.

"My ex barely even talks to me anymore," said Simon. "If I get a 'hi' when I'm picking up my daughter, it's an anomaly." He sat back in his chair, fooling with the blinds on the window next to him. It looked out into the ER hallway.

Buzz.

"*Oh, Jesus! Are you okay?*" she wrote.

"*No worse for the wear.*" He returned his attention to Simon. "Our wives must've gone to the same conference."

"First they hate you," said Simon. "Then they want the kid to hate you. Before you know it, you're defending yourself to an eight-year-old." He flung the cord. "I mean, for fuck's sake, our problems had nothing to do with the kid."

Buzz.

"*Were you able to find him?*" she asked.

He tapped his fingers quickly across the screen as Simon continued complaining about his ex-wife. "*I'd like to talk in person.*"

Buzz.

"*I can meet you somewhere.*"

He nodded along while Simon spoke, feigning interest in the subject.

"*Can you find some time tomorrow night?*" he sent back.

"… thing I want is a battle, you know?"

Arthur was staring straight through Simon. He blinked out of his stupor. "Yeah, you've got that right." Again, he lightly caressed the knot on his forehead. This time he winced. It was tender.

Friday, October 9, 2015, 8:05 PM

He was right there to open the door when Codi knocked. She was wearing a knit shawl, trying to fight off the chill. "Almost time for jackets," he said.

"Most of mine are already out." She stepped through the threshold and ran her fingers through her hair, which had blown wild from the wind. Arthur took the shawl from her hands and folded it neatly, draping it over the back of the couch. She winced as he turned to face her. "My God, Arthur." She admired the bulging lump on his forehead.

He ran his fingers over it. "I feel like I'm growing another head."

"How's your ear?" she asked, inadvertently clenching her fists in reaction to looking at the raised flesh.

"A bit muffled." He gently pressed the soft tissue under his right ear. "It doesn't hurt. And there's no more ringing."

"*How?*" she asked.

"Come on in." He motioned to the kitchen. "I'll tell you."

Codi sat on the same chair Sarah had occupied a week earlier. "Would you like something to drink?" he asked, taking a beer from the refrigerator. She asked for water. "How's your daughter?" He twisted open the cap and handed her the bottle.

"Good. Getting big."

He thought of May, barely able hold herself up

while sitting, her head bobbing as if on a spring. He'd imagined for so long what her little voice would sound like. Calling him Daddy. Dad, eventually. Would her voice be a tad gruff like his? Or would she have the singsong tone of her mother? Light and airy, the emotion always obvious, as if always on the verge of tears, happy or sad. He pulled up a chair and sat too.

"It's a nice place," she said. "How long have you been here?"

He flipped through his mind. "Five years? Coming up on five years. Was a shithole when we bought it. Previous owner was a smoker and had what I can only assume was a thousand cats. I think they used the floor as their litter box."

She cringed.

"We had to rip up every floorboard on this first floor. Luckily, they didn't destroy the upstairs, disgusting creatures."

"I hate them," Codi said. "They're sneaky and finicky and serve no purpose. They eat, kick litter all over, and then sleep all day. When they're not moaning about something, that is. Or scratching your ankles until they bleed." She paused for his reaction. There was none. "We had a cat growing up and I had to change the box – that was my chore."

"Miserable."

"Yes."

He drank from his brown bottle.

"So where did you find him?" she asked.

"Who?"

"John Braun."

He was relieved she had bought it up. He so badly wanted to tell her about the field. Because he trusted her, he recognized. And also because there was no one else to tell. "His way of speaking threw me for a loop, as you said it did to you."

"Kind of hypnotizing," Codi said. "The way a good narrator is."

"He was restless, though," said Arthur. "Nothing like you'd described him. He was looking over his shoulder the entire time."

"I guess you would be too if everyone thought you were out of your mind."

"Better than when *you* believe you're out of your mind." For as close as he'd come to believing it all, he was treading the fine line of feeling insane. And if anyone managed to tell him as much, he would probably believe them, and he could not have that. "After confiding in him and showing him I didn't believe him to be just another loony, he came around. Turns out he was pretty passionate about this himself. Learning the history and whatnot."

"Why?" she asked.

"Because he was a victim when he was younger."

The thermostat kicked on.

"And now he's got some sort of attraction," Arthur continued. "Like he's the poster boy. And I know he's tired of it, but he feels compelled to help. Not, like, morally or anything, I don't think. He *needs* to help."

"So he just waits for people?" Codi asked, her nose crinkling, the freckles bunching into one place.

"I don't know if it's him waiting as much as it is him being forced to stay. I don't know why. I don't think he knows why."

She shifted in her seat.

"He also told me that none of the abducted seem to remember their disappearance."

Codi blurted, "You know, I didn't find Cara at the front door."

Arthur wrinkled his forehead.

"When I called the police to tell them she'd been returned home, I told them she was at the front door. She was actually tucked into her bed, sound asleep. Like nothing had ever happened.

"I snatched her up, squeezed her tight. I stripped her of all her clothes and checked her tiny body up and down. But there was nothing out of place. She woke without recognition of anything abnormal, other than me scaring the crap out of her. The police arrived really quickly, and I walked down to the front hallway so they wouldn't find me in her room. They swarmed the house with squad cars, sirens blaring, which did not help her relax, but I cradled her close and they canvased the grounds outside, trying to find the invisible man.

"They came in and searched the house from top to bottom. Then they took us to the hospital and ran a full battery of tests on her. Physicals, blood work, you name it. While a doctor tended her, the police questioned me. Finally, they let us go home."

"She never remembered anything of being gone?"

Codi shook her head. "She didn't say much the first day home, only cuddled close and grabbed at me constantly, not wanting to be put down. Still, no recollection of anything from what I could see. It wasn't until the second day that I was able to bring myself to ask her if she remembered Mommy not being with her at all recently. She rejected the idea in any way she knew how to express, and has continued to do so any other time I've asked. But who knows? She was so young. Could've seemed like a dream. A nightmare." She ran her fingers along the grain of the table. "I expected the police to pester me for a long time. Even charge me with something. The fear of my daughter being taken away from me again kept me up most nights. But the police never came. All was quiet, even when my family and friends weren't. The looks and muffled chatter was everywhere. The few friends who hadn't bought into it disclosed all this to my parents and me. Instead of fighting to vindicate myself to them all, to those I had loved and who I thought loved me, I decided to bow out. Let the chatterers chatter. I had my daughter. I'd been alone the entire time. I didn't need them anymore."

Arthur thought of Sarah. "Some people just can't handle it. Although," he touched his chest, "am I really even handling it?"

"Better than I did."

"I *highly* doubt that." He pointed to the aching lump on his forehead and then dropped his hand to his lap.

"Again, *how?*"

"John told me about a place in the woods," Arthur said.

"What do you mean?" Codi asked, shifting again in her seat.

"He asked me to stop at this patch of land somewhere in Vance Park." He rocked back on the hind legs of the chair and balanced. "Right off a local road in the middle of the woods."

"And you went? Alone?"

"Well, I went looking for it and, when I found it, I had to check it out. Couldn't resist. Morbid curiosity, call it." His justification felt weak. It seemed dopey that he had decided to venture in by himself. "I pulled onto the shoulder. The sun was all but gone at that point, but I figured I would just poke my head in. I honestly didn't know how far I'd go, just that I'd check things out. Then the ringing started." He pointed to his ear. "You know when you're in a quiet room and you hear that whine? It was like that but got worse the farther I walked. So I got the hell out of there." His face hardened. "It was like something didn't want me around. I thought I was losing it."

The pain in his forehead intensified as the ibuprofen wore off.

"What do you think it was?" she asked.

"Beats me. John mentioned a house on the

property, said something about answers, but I didn't even get far enough to see the clearing."

"Answers," she said.

Arthur shrugged hopelessly. He picked up his beer and pressed it lightly against the bump. The cold glass soothed the throbbing for a moment. "I'm going back."

"I want to go," she said immediately. "Maybe it's not as bad for me, you know? I've already been through it. You're still going through it. Maybe it's worse." Her voice grew with excitement. "I'll bet that's what it is." Arthur was amazed at her motivation for knowing the truth. Here she sat, in his kitchen, her daughter safe and sound at home with her parents, and she was attempting to atone for her sins. Yet it seemed she was there not only for an obligation to what she had done, but also for her own sake. For her own clarity and desire to know the truth. He admired that.

She rose from her chair and snatched the dishtowel hanging from the oven door and pressed the lever on the ice dispenser, filling the center of the towel. She twisted it into a bundle and placed her hand on the back of Arthur's head, gently pushing the makeshift icepack onto the protrusion on his face.

He moaned softly in relief.

"Better?"

He looked up at her and nodded. "Thank you."

She smiled.

The touch of a mother, he thought. "What was it like?

Seeing Cara's face for the first time?"

She shifted her weight from one foot to the other. "Like seeing her born again." She stared straight ahead at the poster hanging on the wall (a vaudevillian show, touring January 21-22-23, 1898) but seeing only her daughter's face, picturing the moment she had reached down and slid both her arms under her child's tiny, sleeping body, pulling Cara snugly against her chest, against her heart. "After a long, painful labor." Her eyes were wet.

"I'm sorry."

She shook her head and rolled her eyes. "No, I'm sorry." She placed the towel full of ice on the table and bent over and hugged him. He dropped the front legs of the chair to the floor, startled. "I'm so sorry."

He placed a hand on the small of her back. "For what?"

"For doing this to you." She sobbed and took his face in both of her hands, squatting to his level. Her nails were a deep blue, like the sky when the sun is just about gone. He could smell her perfume, floral, close to something his mother would wear. The contact of her skin sent waves through his body. He hadn't been touched by anyone in months. "You didn't deserve this," she said in a tiny but determined voice. "You're a good person." She closed her eyes.

Arthur lifted her chin. "You didn't deserve it either."

"I did. I deserved it for this. I was this type of person before. It was in me to do something like this all along. I deserved it. I deserve it."

"We're here now," he said. "This is what it is, so we're going to figure it out." He wiped a tear from her cheek with the back of his tattooed knuckles, the letters M-A-Y followed by a heart inscribed across them.

She put her hands on his shoulders now. He could feel her warm palms through the fabric of his shirt. "I promise you that I will help you get through this, any way that I have to." She stood abruptly. "I brought the binder for you to keep. It's in my car. I'll get it before I leave. I don't know if it will be of use to you, but you're more than welcome to it." She breathed deeply. "I should get going."

Arthur blinked away the moment and followed her to the living room.

She unfurled her shawl and draped it across her shoulders. "When do you plan on going back?"

"This weekend." He pulled the shawl straight. "Codi, I really don't think you should come. I'm not sure how safe it is. Look." He gestured to his face. "You've got your daughter to worry about. Getting yourself hurt for no reason isn't smart."

"It's not for no reason," she said, curling her lips into a humorless smile. "I've got some unfinished business, too. And two heads are better than one."

"Two-and-a-half," Arthur corrected, again looking at the knot from under his brow. "Maybe a full three by the time we go."

"Don't sleep on your face," Codi said, twisting

the knob. She turned back and stared him in the eyes before hugging him tightly once more. A desperate hug. She had no one, she had said it herself, and Arthur could feel that in her embrace. She made herself out to be a loner, but everyone craves affection. Yet her desire was wrapped in the guilt of her past, where she sold someone else's heart for access to her own. She was broken all over with small pieces floating around inside, desperate to find a way to put them back together.

He wrapped his arms around her.

"Please let me know when you go," she said, releasing him. He nodded, and she pulled open the door. "I'll run the book in."

Saturday, October 10, 2015, 1:51 AM

The walls appeared stark white in the soft lamplight from atop May's espresso-colored dresser and faded to pastel pink as the strength of the bulb diminished toward the ceiling. The mobile of stuffed birds and flowers danced ever-so-gently from the subtle draft pressing through the house, casting shadows on the wall that grew and shrunk with each sway.

He spoke aloud to May, as he did most nights, telling her how much closer he was to bringing her home. He told her about his day, what was new, and how he could not wait to hold her again, to feel her burrow her face in his shoulder like she always did. He also told May how much her mother loved her.

When he was done, he shut off the light and closed the door behind him, making his way to the guest bedroom where he'd been sleeping. The binder was splayed across the mattress, open to the middle page with the front half crushing his pack of cigarettes. He stubbed the one in his hand in the ashtray on the nightstand and thumbed through the plastic-sleeved pages. Codi had printed, cut, and pasted sections of articles onto white Xerox paper.

Local Boy Found Alive In Basement After Four Months Missing

Toddler Goes Missing Moments After What Parents Describe As Wailing Sound

Infant Discovered In Car Seat After Three Months Missing

Four, five, six pages full of newspaper trimmings, askew against the white behind them. The fonts and clarity from scanned pages and digital copies changed as the years progressed. Most were sequential, resulting in a chain of events over the last hundred-plus years, all linked in their own deranged and unique way. Codi had done her homework thoroughly.

What was glaringly obvious, however, was a gap

of forty-nine years, from October 31, 1932, when missing child Lester Scott, 9, of Perkasie, Pennsylvania was found asleep in his bed, to October 20, 1981, when David Leach of Richlandtown, Pennsylvania went missing while in the bathroom of a Sizzler. He was found a year later, in the same bathroom.

Forty-nine years. Either it had gone dormant or, more likely, Codi was not able to find the correlating cases. Perhaps they were ambiguous in their descriptions. Or not reported at all.

Arthur finished his beer and placed it on the nightstand next to countless other empties. He got out of bed and pulled the bottom sheet taught on the mattress and then fluffed the comforter, but the room spun, and he tossed himself, stomach-down, onto the pillow top and crawled underneath the blanket, careful to turn his head to the side, avoiding the knot. His arms and legs dangled from the full-sized bed.

As he dozed, his phone vibrated next to him on the mattress. He leaned it toward his face and squinted at the brightness.

The text message read, "*Are you okay?*"

"*No,*" he answered. He scratched his chin through the whiskers, which were no longer rough but had softened with growth. "*But thank you for coming tonight.*" He sent it without hesitation. It was not the liquor. It was not the exhaustion. It was the truth. He felt better after seeing Codi, and he was not sorry for that. Not at first.

"What do you mean?"

He blinked and lifted his chin from the bed. It churned the countless beers. He gagged but kept the contents down.

What was she asking? He meant what he had said. Did it not come across that way? Fucking text messages.

"Arthur, are you drunk?"

He read it slowly, not sure what to make of it. He burped a mouthful of partially digested beer and swallowed it faster than he could react. Had he drank too much while she was there? A bottle or two, he figured. Couldn't have been much more than that.

She could be assuming that he was drunk, to say something like he did. She wouldn't be wrong.

"No. Not really …" he began typing when he noticed the name.

Sarah.

He closed his eyes tightly. That's when the rest of the night's indulgences found their way up his esophagus and into the back of his throat. He sprung from the bed and through the door, thunking against the frame on his way. He sprayed the hallway wall with vomit before clapping a hand over his mouth and rumbling into the bathroom. He dropped onto his knees with a thud before the toilet. The rest flowed like a river and was emptied in less than a minute. He dropped onto his rear and his back came to rest catty-corner between the wall and the bathtub.

The room looked different. Brighter. It spun

again and the knot on his forehead ached terribly from the pressure of the blood racing to his head.

Slowly, everything returned to focus. Arthur panted and rubbed his stomach. After a time, he stood and stumbled back to the bed, where he forgot about his phone.

7.

"Hello?"

"Hi, Sarah, it's me."

"Arthur." She paused. He could hear she was driving. *"How's the hangover?"*

He rubbed the back of his neck. "Sarah, I'm sorry. I got out of control last night. I drank a lot." There was no way he could afford to have Sarah believing he was speaking with another woman, let alone Codi. "I was hammered when I got your messages." He bit the bullet. "I was out cold and must have been dreaming. And then the text message woke me up to a stupor. It felt so real that I just answered you that way. Just perfect timing, I guess." He stopped at an intersection as the cars whizzed by Bridge Street. The day was warm enough to walk to work, and a sweatshirt with sleeves pushed up and sunglasses for the clear skies (and for the hangover) sufficed. A car

144

waved him through, and he crossed the crosswalk.

"So you're still drinking."

"Not often," he lied. "Just after a long day." He made it to the sidewalk and continued to West Mechanic Street.

"I spoke with Mason the other day," she said. *"He tells me you're barely in the shop anymore."*

Arthur exhaled sharply. Something broke inside of him. "Really? Because I'm just about out front now. I can shoot you a picture if you'd like. Hang on, let me get the camera open."

"That's fine, Arthur."

"No, I mean, you like to keep tabs on me. Let me at least make you look like a fool."

"Excuse me?" Her voice was dry.

"I'm sorry Sarah, did I offend you? Am I a child? Do you need to keep an eye on me? Why not just call me directly?"

"I did-"

"You walk out on me when I need you most," he interrupted. "You rip whatever was left of my heart out and step on it, then you continue to fuck with me on the rare occasion you feel like picking up the phone. I'm not supposed to be upset?"

"I did it-"

"I don't care why you did it. You and your reasons. Your ever-important reasons. It's your world, Sarah, and we're all just living in it, right? You're the only one who's lost a child. The only one who's going through hell." He stood in front of the shop and absentmindedly watched Mason and Nayeli work. Someone sat in the waiting area, the back of his head to the window. He licked his finger and paged through a magazine. "We should all cater to you. I'm sure your parents are. Your whole family must think what an asshole I turned out to be, huh?"

"Arthur." This time she raised her voice. *"I did it because I love you."*

He laughed once. "Oh, you love me. You love me. You guys hear that?" he yelled. "My wife, who left me just a few months after my daughter was *kidnapped*, loves me. She even checked in on me! Son of a bitch, Sarah, I have to say … thank you. Thank you for loving me. God, I've never felt more content." By now, the entire shop had taken notice and everyone was watching the show. The few straggling pedestrians had crossed the street. He inhaled deeply, filling his lungs with crisp air scented with abscission and ozone. *You're going too far,* he thought. "You're hurting me, Sarah. I don't want to keep hurting."

The line was quiet but she was still there, listening.

He wiped his eyes. "I'm tired of pain. You don't get used to it. You don't live with it. I drown it in any way that I can. If that's by reading whatever I can get my hands on, calling the station, or drinking a case, then that's what I'm going to do."

"You don't think I'm hurting?" she asked.

"I never said that. Why would I? Is this a

contest?"

"No, it's not, but everyone handles pain differently. Seeing you destroy yourself was hurting me. Why do you think I left? Because I don't love you? Because I don't want to be with you? Of course I do. I miss our home. I miss our life. I miss you!"

He sat down on the concrete steps next to the store. They led to an alleyway beside the building, where another storefront emerged from an underground entrance. "Then come home."

"I can't."

He leaned against the structure. It was the same story, over and over again.

"I can't just watch you unravel. I'm not going to contribute to it."

"I'm going to find her," he said dejectedly. He wanted to tell her, not to give her solace but to stick it to her. To say *I told you so.* A big middle finger. To his daughter's mother, the woman he loved more than any other. The one he agreed to spend the rest of his life with. The thought of purposely spiting her was unsettling, but it was real. "I'm close."

"And I pray it happens," she said.

"You don't have to believe me. I don't need you to. But what then, Sarah? What happens when I find our daughter? You'll come crawling back, won't you? Or will you try to take her from me?"

"I'm going to go," she said. *"I'm driving, and I need to pay attention."*

"Then pay attention."

"I love you, Arthur. Please, please take care of yourself."

"You'll regret this."

"Goodbye."

"Sarah. Sarah, don't hang up-"

The call disconnected. Arthur looked at the phone, which returned him to the home screen. May stared back at him with a big, toothless grin.

1:25 PM

"Jesus, Arthur," said Nayeli. "Your face."

The knot had reduced in size a tiny bit, but the purple and black bruise on and around it had spread onto his temple, the bridge of his nose, and up his forehead."

"You sure you can tattoo?" she asked.

"I'm good," Arthur said. "To be honest, I need to right now."

Not everything had gone to hell. On a Friday, just after one in the afternoon, both artists had clients in their seats and a walk-in waiting on the bench. It had been busy, according to Nayeli and the books. With requests for Arthur put on indefinite hold, he had been afraid the business would take a hit, but his employees were remarkable in their own right, and that led to a self-sustaining environment, provided all were happy. And they seemed to be. Mason had just gotten married a few weeks before. Alejandro and his wife welcomed their second born, another boy. That part of his life, albeit small, was the one constant. He missed being there every day. The late nights, finishing a six-hour piece, the front door open and the breeze billowing in, he missed it all terribly. He missed the normality it represented most of all. The pictures that Sarah used to send him of May being bathed. The calls from her telling him that she was going to sleep, but that she loved him with all of her heart. Every night. She loved him every night. That was special.

"I won't take him," he said, gesturing to the man waiting on the bench. "He watched me lose my shit outside. He's going to be looking in the mirror the entire time, making sure I don't shank him or something."

Nayeli snickered. "I'll be done with Alyssa over there in twenty minutes. It's a few numbers on her ankle. I'll let the gentleman know."

"Good deal."

He settled in, clearing his mind. Two hours later, a woman in her early twenties walked in asking to make an appointment. She wanted a pinwheel on her shoulder. Arthur decided to freehand it and tattoo her right then and there.

"Ambitious," Nayeli said from her chair.

"I got it." He flexed his left fist, loosening the healing skin over his knuckles before pulling on the black, sterile glove.

"You were right," Mason said ten minutes later, leaning over Arthur's shoulder, scoping out the hand-drawn stencil on the woman's shoulder. "That's nice."

Arthur made short work of the piece. He hadn't missed a beat.

"I want to thank you guys," he said between clients. The store was empty, aside from a man in Mason's chair. "You held it down for me. You're *holding* it down for me. I really don't know how to thank you enough." He ran his hand through his hair, slicking it back into place. "I'm lucky to have you. And the other two schnooks, too."

"With what you're going through," Nayeli said, "you do what you have to do. We're here no matter what, you know that."

Arthur nodded thankfully and leaned back in his chair. He rubbed his face with both hands.

"Next time I'll tell Sarah you've been here, though," Mason said after a moment.

"Please do," Arthur said from under his palms. It deadened the words.

A few more hours went by, this time without a client. Arthur filled the gap by talking with his two employees, catching up on their lives. More than great workers, they were two of the nicest people he had the pleasure of knowing. In the tattoo world, that was not always the case. Divas and drama. And gruff old assholes. The only issue he had with his two employees were how good they were, and he knew it was only a matter of time before they would go off on their own. And for as much as he dreaded that day, he would welcome it with open arms because they deserved it. Particularly Nayeli, who wrung her heart into every tattoo, injecting a small piece of her soul with each one. And it showed.

Arthur was dozing in the drawing chair when the front door startled him awake. Nayeli was halfway through a three-hour session and Mason had left to pick up dinner. The sun had just about set, and the time difference made him feel like a toddler waking in a different bed. *Where the heck am I?*

"I'm Arthur," he said, bobbing to the front of the shop and extending his hand to the man who'd walked in.

"Anthony," the gentleman said in a gruff voice. He was a large, hefty man with a buzzed head and a goatee.

"What can I do for you today, Anthony?"

"I'm looking to get this tattooed on my arm." He slid Arthur a photograph of another man's tattoo. It was an anchor on the forearm. At least, it looked like an anchor. It was so faded and weathered that Arthur couldn't tell for sure. "That there's my dad," Anthony said. "I want to get what he had, just modern and clear-like, ya know?"

It gave Arthur pause.

"Do you think you can do it?"

"I'd be honored. You up for getting tattooed now?"

"That'd be great, brother! Man, I was afraid I'd'a had to come back."

"You're in luck today. Give me a few minutes to draw it up. I'll make it out as best I can and then we can tweak it if need be."

"Do your thing, Arthur," he said.

"Hang over there on the seats. I'll call you on back when I'm ready."

A half-hour later, Arthur was applying the ointment and getting ready for the first line.

"So is your dad still with us?" he asked.

"No, sir. He passed a few years ago."

"Sorry to hear that."

Mason returned with a few cups of coffee and his meal.

"Ah, he suffered, man. It's better. Diabetic. Had throat cancer at the end. Just a mess. All them years smoking will do that to you."

Arthur glanced down at the shape of the pack of cigarettes in his breast pocket. "So I've heard."

"You oughta think about quittin'. I'll tell you a thousand stories that'll make your cheeks clench. Though I'll bet you've heard a lot of them before," he said. "Sometimes it just don't matter until that person is good and ready, right? Or dead. Or dyin'. But then it's too late. I watched my pops go through it and boy was I glad I put it down."

"Was he a military man?"

"Navy. Career."

"Wow. And you?"

Anthony looked at Arthur. He didn't have much of a neck. A naturally stocky man, though a few years in the gym might've exaggerated that. His arms were gigantic, though not especially defined, just large and alabaster in color. "Did my four, twenty years ago now. Didn't have it in me to go the distance. I'm not as good a man as pops was."

"Sounds like your dad was a hell of a guy. I'm sure he'd appreciate this."

"He always wanted to get his redone," said Anthony.

"Really?"

"Yeah, but with the diabetes and everything else, he was nervous to do it. I told him he still could, but he was a stubborn dude."

"Where'd he get his tattoo done?"

"Off the ship somewhere in Cali. These guys used to set up their shops right near bases. Military guys were like the only ones getting inked at the time, so they went where the money was."

"Kind of like the Girl Scout who sets up shop in front of the college dorm."

Nayeli cracked up from her chair.

"Yes sir," Anthony said. "Knew their audience!"

"I've heard they used to tattoo each other," Arthur said, recalling what John Braun had told him. "The servicemen, that is."

"That's what the old guy used to say. I don't know how true it was. Probably, though. Them guys were fuckin' nuts."

Mason placed a cup of coffee on Arthur's table.

"Thanks, bud. I needed a boost." Arthur dipped the needle in the ink. "Start yer engines," he said, revving his machine. "I'm going to make a line,

Anthony. Let me know if it's okay for you." He lowered the machine and blasted the ink into Anthony's arm. The black pigment pooled around the short line until Arthur wiped it away.

"Just fine," Anthony said.

"You picked a good spot for your first," Arthur said. "Upper arm isn't too bad. We'll do your ribs next time."

Anthony let out some air. "That bad there, huh?"

"I puked," Mason said from the front desk. His back was to everyone as he scarfed down a steak sandwich.

"No shit?" Anthony said.

"Sure did. Five-hour session. I just internalized all the pain, went home to take a shower, and barfed in my bathtub." He turned around and lifted his shirt to display an Oni mask spanning eight inches from top to bottom, nearly covering the entire left side of his ribcage.

"Gorgeous, brother," Anthony said.

"Right on, man. Thank you."

Arthur continued tattooing. "I had to stop about thirty times. And mine is half the size of his."

Mason said something, but Arthur locked in on the line he was drawing. Background noise faded into the distance as he watched his hand trace the outline onto Anthony's large arm. It was as if he had taken a step out of his body and was watching as an outsider. He forgot how to tattoo in that moment, but the Arthur in control of the machine was a master. He guided it with ease, deft and controlled. The Arthur on the outside marveled at the precision, but it was the artwork itself that ultimately enamored him. Everything was slow. Mason and Anthony conversed in the distance, but nothing was more important than the ink. Than the anchor. The anchor was familiar. Like he had known it his entire life.

The needle punched, now even slower, through the skin, spraying tiny droplets of ink and plasma into the air. Each pierce was a fresh wound, hundreds per second, obliterating the cells of the body, scarring it forever.

The anchor was all that existed then. It meant something. It meant everything. But the Arthur outside of his real body could not comprehend why. The Arthur inside his body was on autopilot.

Arthur Outside turned to face Arthur Inside. He stared at the man who was a shell of his former self. Grays were rampant on his scalp and face. The bags under his eyes were puffy and dark, nearly black in contrast with the pale complexion surrounding them. His lips were a straight line. The muscles near his jaw clenched on and off as he worked, focus and absentmindedness combined. His neck was a network of pronounced veins and skin wrapped tightly around bone, his Adam's apple protruding. This was a beaten man, and he suddenly felt a great sadness for Arthur Inside.

"Never feel sorry for yourself," his mother used to tell him. "That's when apathy rears its ugly head and you start to give up." God, he missed her. She would have been here with him. She would not have left when things got hard. Instead, she would have pushed him. Told him she was proud of him for fighting so goddamn hard. For taking the responsibility onto his own shoulders. When his dad left, she did not look in the mirror and cry. Never. She pressed on, and made things better.

Make things better.

He moved closer, nose-to-nose, looking himself in the eyes, and then turned back to the tattoo. The outline was taking shape, and an anchor was discernable.

"*Not much left to it now, but the memories are there all the same.*" John Braun's voice played through Arthur's mind like a recording. He remembered John's own anchor, barely recognizable. The same tattoo, so vague and indistinguishable, was now being tattooed on Anthony's arm by Arthur Inside, just as washed out and weathered.

No, don't do that, Arthur Outside thought. *That's not what the man wants.* But Arthur Inside pressed on, filling in the faded blue that made up the anchor. Arthur Outside stared at Arthur Inside. Stared him up and down. *You stupid fuck*, he thought. *What are you doing? What the hell are you doing?* He glanced back, and the anchor was new again, only an outline, crisp and clean and perfect. And done.

"*Because I'm in the club.*"

What, John? What do you want? What do you want here?

"Was it your child?"
"It was me."
It was him.

"When you were a baby?"
"When I was younger."

"Why you?"
"Because I'm in the club. When I was younger. Not much left to it now, but the memories are there all the same.
When he was younger.

Because I'm in the club.
Because I'm in the club.
Because I'm in the club.

The machine buzzed furiously, the voices in the room still a million miles away. Arthur Outside cried hysterically. Arthur Inside tattooed stoically. Then they merged, like two eyes focusing.

Anthony held up the picture of his father in his left hand. Mason asked a question. The distance closed and reality came back into focus. "… big guy, too?"

"When he was younger," said Anthony. "About this age here he was in top shape. He was twenty, you know?" He flipped it around. There was a date on the back. "Yeah, twenty. To be fuckin' twenty again." He shook his head. "He slimmed out as he got older. Then when he got sick, he withered away to nothin'. Was tough to watch."

Arthur stopped. Both Anthony and Mason noticed the wide-eyed look on his face.

"You okay?" asked Mason.

Arthur nodded, blinking it off. "Fine, just remembered something." He continued tattooing Anthony, not saying much until he was finished. Anthony paid, thanked Arthur profusely for the wonderful job, and left.

Arthur was not too far behind, again praising Nayeli and Mason for their efforts at maintaining order. "I won't be in for a few days again. Have some things to take care of. But my phone is always on if you guys need anything."

Nayeli hugged him hard, squeezing his shoulders. "We love you. All of us. You don't need to explain anything. Take all the time you need."

He smiled back at her and then shook Mason's hand. "Thanks. I miss this place." He looked around. "I'll be back, though, for good. Soon."

8:02 PM

Arthur waited until he was clear of the doors before erupting into a sprint down West Mechanic.

The street narrowed after a tenth of a mile, so much so that only the width of a car could fit. The houses turned to bushes and then to trees, and the road resembled a path more than a street. He traveled it every day, so the dark wasn't an issue. He focused ahead, passing the usual landmarks en route to his house. Out of the woods emerged train tracks, parallel to the street. He ran alongside them as he entered another patch of houses. It cut to the right, intersecting with the tracks, and continued northerly until finally turning into South Sugan Road, where he crossed the intersection and cut another right onto Old York Road. He stopped at the corner, sucking in as much air as his lungs would hold. He panted furiously, wheezing, hands on his knees. When he finally caught his breath, he paced slowly through the leaf-covered street. The trees were nearly barren, and his house, white with black shutters, was visible through them even in the night.

He had finally caught his breath by the time he crossed the lawn to the stoop. He tried pulling his keys from his pocket but struggled to free them as they gnarled themselves around the cotton. "Come on!" he shouted at the inanimate objects and pulled firmly until they finally jangled free. He bound through the doorway and up the steps where he crashed into the spare room. At the foot of the bed was the binder. He pulled it close to the edge of the mattress and knelt on the floor next to it. He opened to the same pages he'd been reading the night before.

"David Leach of Richlandtown, Pennsylvania went missing while in the bathroom of a Sizzler," Arthur said to the empty room. "October 20, 1981. The twentieth." He flipped forward until he was close to the end of the book and skimmed the text. "No," he said, flicking to the next page. "No. Not it." He grunted and flipped again. Then it jumped up at him.

CRUX, SUNDAY, OCTOBER 20, 1981 – Richard Porter, 94, died at home early Sunday morning.

October twentieth.

"My son is still alive. Please alert the police."

Arthur laughed one loud and sudden yelp.

Porter's son, Daniel John Porter, went missing on Halloween, 1932, or forty-nine years ago next week. The younger Porter was on two-week leave from the Navy and was said to have gone missing from his childhood home.

Arthur dropped onto his haunches, his back to the bed.

"I looked for any records of him once I got home. I found nothing. No proof of a John Braun anywhere in the area. None that matched him, I mean. It's a common name. It blends in. Which is why I believe he made it up. And I know there's more to him than I ever found out."

Daniel John Porter.

Arthur snatched his phone from his back pocket and dialed Codi. It rang once. Twice. He waited patiently, certain the call would go to voicemail.

"Hello?" The voice was groggy and quiet.

"Codi, it's me. Were you asleep?"

She cleared her throat. *"Kind of,"* she whispered. *"Was just getting Cara to sleep. Let me go downstairs."*

He jumped to his feet and paced the room. He wanted to scream, but suppressed the excitement by pulling a cigarette from the box.

"Okay," Codi said, more alert. *"Everything all right?"*

He flicked the spark wheel and lit the tobacco. "John Braun *isn't* his real name," he said after inhaling the smoke. He blew it through his nose and mouth. "It's Daniel Porter, and he went missing in 1932, at the age of twenty."

"I'm confused," she said.

"Codi, Braun is a hundred-and-three years old."

8.

Sunday, October 11, 2015, 10:10 AM

Sarah held the picture of May at eye-level, her elbow supported on the ledge of the piano. She plunked a few keys with her opposite hand. Sheet music, either her mother's or father's, sat open on the rack. Sarah had never gotten much further than grade school talent level, though she constantly reminded Arthur of her desire to play again. He, in turn, professed his desire to learn the drums. Then they would both list dozens of other things they aspired to learn, restricted by the constraints of having a family, working, and making sure to have enough time for their own company. The latter suffered periodically but was never really too much of an issue. The less time they had to spend together, the more they made it count. Nothing kept them from each other. Not from the moment they met.

And now it was all different and Sarah was the

reason for that. She struggled to deal with that control. She could numb the pain just by getting in the car and driving home. Numb it for how long, though? The wound was festering, and eventually nothing would make the hurt go away.

She had always heard of couples crumbling after losing a child and never understood why. Marriage is constant. The love of a child is separate. Just as strong, if not stronger, but different, nonetheless. One should not affect the other. It was a morbid thought, but more children could be had. You would be sad, mourn, and move on as best you could.

But she understood now. The child becomes part of the fabric, making up just as much of the whole as any other part. When they are gone, when that seam splits, and part of the fabric is torn away, the entire thing can fall apart. Arthur had fallen apart. Sarah was falling apart. And when the day came that they would find May's body, the entire thing would fall apart.

11:11 AM

Arthur adjusted the heat as Codi flipped through the binder. She lifted her thermos full of coffee from the cup holder between the driver and passenger seats. A Leonard Cohen song played low on the radio. The coffee, still too hot for her lips, billowed steam. She replaced it in the holder, this time leaving it open to cool.

Arthur sat back against the seat, holding the steering wheel with both hands, the bandaged one with a looser grip. The trees whizzed by on Route 223. "That's the turn off," he said softly, pointing at the road leading to the forest.

She nodded and smiled haplessly. "Will we still go?"

He took a moment to think about it. "I think so. I want to hear what John has to say, first." A sprinkling of houses appeared as they closed in on Crux. A lodge here, a small subdivision there and, finally, a fork in the road where 223 hung to the right and civilization came about quickly. Codi sighed. She held both hands between her legs, under the binder, and shivered. Arthur again raised the heat.

"I'm okay," she said, reaching out to turn the knob back to where it was. "I'm always cold, but thank you. How does your face feel?"

The bruise had spread down his cheek and into his hairline, deepening in color. The purple was now violet, with greens and dark reds swirled in.

"Less sore, actually. I look like a freak show."

"Better than feeling like one."

"You're right," he said, smirking. They pulled in front of the five and dime. John was neither out front nor anywhere else, as far as they could see. "Now comes the John Braun hunt. No trip to Crux would be complete without one."

"Luckily for me, this is where I started and finished. Found him first try." She stared at where the table had been, taken inside, presumably for the cold weather season.

"Are you okay to be here?" asked Arthur.

"I'm okay," she said, still looking through the window.

"I think I'll try the old inn again," he said, pulling back onto the street, heading for the intersection where West Broad Street veered left and into a U-turn.

"Is that him?" Codi asked excitedly. "Over there." She pointed her red fingernail at a building on the corner, another inn. Arthur snapped his head to the passenger window. He quickly pulled his car to the curb and hopped out, walking to the front and staring at the back of the person loitering on the steps of the building, about twenty-five yards away. It was John, all right. He and Delilah were taking residence in front of the side entrance. The entire place looked almost abandoned. John and his dog faced the opposite direction, standing next to one of the few planter boxes that were placed in odd locations around the brick foundation. An overhang with handrails bordered the second story above him, though there were no doors, rendering the entire thing practically useless. The word HOTEL was painted in block letters between the second and third (and topmost) story, with an illuminated VACANT sign in the window facing that side of the street. The lights were on, but Arthur was doubtful that anyone was home.

"Hi, Daniel." He spoke just loud enough to be heard.

For a moment, John Braun had no reaction. Then he turned around slowly. The passenger door of the car closed as Codi stepped out onto the sidewalk.

"Arthur," he said, surprised, his tone pleasant until he found Arthur's face, when the words clicked. He looked down and then at the building. "Why would you call me that?"

Arthur moved even closer, closing the distance almost completely. "Because that's your name, isn't it?"

John began to cry. "I haven't been called that name in a very long time."

Codi came up beside Arthur. An American flag flapped from a pole on the corner of the intersection. She pulled her fleece coat tighter, nestling her neck and chin into the thick collar.

"You're working together?" John asked, suddenly bright and cheery. "Yes! This, this is it. This is what we need!" He wiped tears from his cheeks with the fingers of his gloves.

Codi, moving only her eyes, took a quick glance at Arthur. "What do you mean?" she asked.

John lurched forward and hugged Arthur, wrapping his long arms around Arthur's shoulders. Arthur could feel whiskers on his ear and let out a surprised grunt. John pulled off and held him by his upper arms. "You're even more intuitive than I'd hoped. Now you can help. You can help me."

"How can he help you?" Codi asked.

"By going to my house."

"Your house?" said Arthur.

"Yes, my house." John smiled. He let go of Arthur's arms. "What was once my house."

"What are you talking about?" Delilah sniffed Arthur's ankles. He paid no mind.

"Well, it was never *really* mine. My father purchased the land in the twenties or thirties, before the park was established. When I needed a place to live and my father was gone, I took residence there for a few years. I'm not one-hundred percent sure who the estate was supposed to go to, but it was abandoned when I got there."

"So that's where you wanted me to go?" said Arthur.

"Yes."

"Why not just tell me?"

John shrugged. "Why not just tell anyone? Let the old stewbum coot look even crazier!" His eyes flared with vim. For the time being, he was twenty again. He was allowed to be. The secret had been shared, Arthur and Codi were in the know, and John could be himself. *Daniel* could be himself."

"So instead, you let me go into the woods without a clue," Arthur said, bitterness in his voice. "You let me get bombarded by … whatever the fuck that was." He raised his hand to his face.

"It did *that* to you?" John was appalled. "It doesn't do that. I've never seen it do something-"

"It happened after," Arthur interrupted.

"After what?" John asked.

"The ringing, the screeching. It turned me away from the field before I had half a chance to go in. It burst my eardrum."

John closed his eyes. "Arthur, I'm sorry. I didn't think that would happen. Whenever anyone has ever gone in, they turn around when it gets too bad. It's never gotten to that," he said, examining the bruise with his eyes.

"Why didn't you tell me?" Arthur asked again.

"Because it seems to be worse when you expect it," he said. "I've tried everything. This time I'd hoped for something different. You seemed ... different." He gave a tug on the leash as Delilah tried to chase a leaf. "I thought maybe it wouldn't affect you as badly. You're strong. And maybe you're more susceptible to it because of that. You cannot go back into those woods. You cannot go near those woods. You're too close as it is. When you leave Crux, don't come back."

"We're going after we leave you," Arthur said.

"Good."

"To the woods," Codi added.

"No." John flicked his eyes back and forth between the two standing in front of him. "I need you to listen to me now. It is pointless. You will only get yourselves even more screwed up." He pointed to his head.

"I want to know what's in that house," Arthur said.

Codi shivered in the breeze.

"There might not even be a house there anymore." John ran his hand down his braid.

"What are you talking about?" Arthur asked.

"I never burned my journals," John admitted with a deep breath. "I told you I had, but I never did. They are on the property, buried under the house."

Arthur wrinkled his eyebrows. "You just said the house might not be there anymore. Why haven't you gone to get them yourself?"

"I can't, for the same reason as you. It won't let me." He leaned back onto the stair rail. "It doesn't hurt. Not physically. But the thoughts and visions, they're horrible. Disorienting. I can barely walk onto the property, never mind make my way to the house."

"But you lived there," Codi said. "Why the change?"

"I got too close."

"To *what?*" Arthur snapped, tired of beating around the bush. "Tell us what you know, John."

John opened his mouth to speak just as a police car slowed next to them.

"What's going on?" the officer asked, lowering his window.

"We're fine," Arthur answered sharply.

"John, you bothering these folks?"

"No, sir." He pulled Delilah close.

"I said we're fine," Arthur said, raising his voice. Codi reached down and took him by the wrist.

The cop stared for a few seconds before raising

his window and continuing on, barely peeling his eyes away from the three of them.

"It was Halloween and I was getting sloshed with some old high school buddies," John said, watching the squad car drive away. "They were barely twenty years old, most of them. Alcohol was illegal, but we managed to get our hands on some, as almost anyone could at the time. Prohibition was practically dead. I wasn't around to see the repeal, but you could feel it coming. Not to mention, back then, if someone in the service was throwing back a few, no one was going to give them hell.

"We were drinking wine, me, George, Hank, and the rest, in the living room of my parents' house. My folks were upstairs in their bedroom and didn't particularly care if we imbibed, they were just nervous of us doing silly things, so we promised them we'd stay home. We had done plenty of silly things in high school – enough to last a lifetime. We just wanted to chew the fat and hang out. Take it easy. I had been stationed in Norfolk at the time and the work was hard. Once I was on my two-week leave, I just wanted to relax. Everyone else was out at Halloween parties, and there we were at home, laughing until we couldn't breathe.

"One minute I'm in the kitchen getting a snack, the next I'm lying on the floor in someone *else's* kitchen. It's 1981, my father is dead, my mother is dead, and I'm believed to be *long* dead."

"I told people who I was and ended up in a

holding cell for the night. It went on like that for a few months until I figured out how to exist on my own. I took my middle name and added the surname from some newspaper article I had been reading. It was inconspicuous, and I could get away with it. I have gotten away with it. John Braun, for all intents and purposes, *is* my name."

Codi edged closer to Arthur.

"I took residence in that house for a few years. It was a dump and falling apart, but look at me." He held out his hands. "A dump, and falling apart. I was broke, alone, and didn't have much of a choice. I could hide out, go unnoticed, so I did just that for a few years. In the beginning, things were boring and typical. I looked for work, did odd jobs here and there, but had a lot of trouble acclimating to modern life. It was a shock. The cars, the music, the technology. The styles. The progressive attitude. I didn't disagree with it," he said. "I just … wasn't used to it. An outcast from the start, John Braun. Some things have just never changed." The wind was sharp, and he zipped up his coat. "I started hearing the voices around that time. At first, they were whispers in the middle of the night, waking me from sleep. I ignored them, refusing to give in to what I truly did not believe in. Odd, isn't it, coming from a man who disappeared for half a century? I guess I just didn't want to let myself believe it. But after a few weeks, it got worse. The whispers became words, and the words became yells and shouts. I began keeping a journal of what I heard. That was the first of many journals.

"I noticed that the voices would cease upon leaving the area, and return in full-force when I would return. So I continued documenting. With what I had been through, and without much to live for, I decided to try to understand what was happening. And what had happened to me." His shoes slid against the cement as he fidgeted his position. "I fought through and recorded everything that was happening. That's when it got worse. Much worse." His eyes were open but he was lost in thought. "At first, I thought they were visions or hallucinations. Eventually, I realized they were memories of a life I did not remember living. Of the abduction. Of what happened to me while I was gone. And memories of *him*. His face, bright red and dripping with sweat, staring at me non-stop. He would grimace and laugh." John's face twisted. "He would cry. Like I was on the other side of his mirror, being forced to observe all of his pain. All of his torment. It happened mostly during the night at first, but eventually spilled over into the day. I would force myself out of the house, leaving the area completely. But something compelled me to go back. The journals, sure, but there was something else. A desire. A need to learn. I wanted more than anything to find out who he was, and who did this to me, and *why*. And the voices, not always the same, told me everything they could. Told *me*, called my name. Referred to me, confessing the sins of someone else.

Describing in detail so many horrible things. That's when it became violent. A man, the same man with the red face, beating a child with a piece of wood, the leg of a table. It was always too dark to see the boy's face, but the screams were always the same. The abrupt last gurgle of life. Finally, silence.

"There were so many others, but I can't remember them. Not the details." He closed his eyes, pinching moisture from them. "One night in particular, it was so horrible that I couldn't stand on my feet. I grabbed my sack of belongings and crawled out of the house. Something begged me, trying desperately to pull me back in. It wasn't malicious, perhaps just desperate. I don't think it wanted to kill me, but it wanted something. Eventually, I dragged myself far enough through the woods to be able to stand up. I stumbled, walked, and then ran as far away as I could. I was young then, in biological terms, at least." He smirked. "I moved fast. By the time I was just about in town, I realized that I'd forgotten my journals. I'd left them under the house, where I kept them secure in a metal box, buried in the dirt under a few loose boards in the center of the floor. I knew that at any given time, someone could go in and bulldoze that house. I wanted to make sure they would be safe, but I could never go back. Never even get close. So there they sit. I hope. I pray."

"Why not bury them somewhere else?" Codi asked.

"I've asked myself the same question, but it came

down to having my things in one place. It's hard to sleep at night when you're entire life is scattered. I had a place to live, so I kept my things there."

"So pay some kid to go in and get them."

"Doesn't work that way. It protects them. I've tried having someone go in after them." He shook his head. "It's just not right putting someone else through it. That's why I believe they're still there."

"And you remember nothing more about them?" Arthur asked.

"I could never remember anything once I'd get a few steps away from the house. The voices, my memories of my being gone, the visions. Everything is in those books. I believe there's some sort of resolution in them, if ever the pieces could be put together, and if ever there was the right person to figure it out." He paused for a moment. "I wouldn't know unless I could go through everything with a sane mind. It doesn't let me leave here, but it keeps me just off my nut enough so that no one takes me seriously. Aside from the select few." He paused again. "It loves the cycle, but it can only keep it going by protecting itself. And that's what the field does. It protects itself. He protects it. And maybe, maybe I wanted to take the books and leave. But maybe it forced me to keep them there. That house. That property. It's the epicenter. Like the nerve running down the middle of whatever this beast is. I think that's why I was attracted to stay there in the first place. I'm not even sure I knew my father had a second house. Why would I know about it? He would take his ladies there. I had no need to know. Yet, I was fully aware of its existence when I came back from wherever I was."

Arthur let go of Codi and reached into his pocket, from which he pulled out a business card. "Do you have a pen?" he asked her. She rummaged through her purse on the passenger seat to get one. "This is my phone number, John," he said, scribbling it on the back of the card. "Use it if you need to. Anything you can think of, anything you need me to know, call me."

John took the card.

"I'm going to get your notebooks, and we're going to figure out how to end this." He turned to walk away.

"Arthur," John said. "Don't wait too long."

Arthur put a hand on the hood of his car and looked back, puzzled.

"For you daughter. Don't wait. You'll ruin her life." He put his hands in his pockets. "I have a sneaking suspicion the longer we're gone, the worse off we are when we get back."

"Why do you think that?" Arthur asked.

"Look at me." He placed his hand on his chest. "Maybe it's incidental, but you'd rather be safe than sorry, right? I've been where you are now, hoping for a resolution. You have me optimistic, Arthur, but the truth is that it's unlikely to be fixed. Look out for your family, first. You don't want your child to end up like me."

Codi was already in the car. She had her head down but heard every word John Braun had to say. She'd heeded his advice once.

"If you wait too long, you risk ruining her like they ruined me. My father waited nearly fifty years to bring me home. My parents made the selfless decision to spare another family the same pain they had to experience. But parents are parents. And even on his deathbed, my father felt the need to give me a chance at life. It just so happens he waited nearly all of his life to pull the trigger. Maybe it was in a deathbed stupor. Maybe it was intentional. Either way, it was wrong.

"If you choose to go that route, just know that you'll spend your entire life second-guessing yourself. It never goes away. Why do you think this still goes on? No one can go through with enduring the loss of a child when they know they can rectify it. It's not in our makeup to sacrifice our own. We protect our own with everything we have, in any way we can. If my father had waited another few minutes, this would probably all be gone."

"We don't know that," Arthur said.

"Not for sure, no. But I would've been better off. And maybe it would've worked."

"Or maybe you would've been stuck there forever, wherever you were."

John gave Delilah a tug. She had fallen asleep at his feet. "Maybe, but who's to say that's not better than a life like this." A cold breeze blew and he looked to the now cloudy sky.

"You serve a greater purpose, John. Look what you've done for us. For Codi. If it weren't for you, we'd be lost."

"If it weren't for me, your daughter would still be here. And Codi's would never have been gone. Then again, there would be someone else, I'm sure," John said, walking away. "He'd make sure of it."

"Who?" Arthur yelled after him. John did not answer.

"Arthur, come on," Codi said from the window. "Leave him."

He got in the car and started the ignition. "Who was he talking about?" he asked, looking blankly at Codi.

"I don't know. But I'll bet whatever is written in those books will tell us."

Arthur pulled away.

12:00 PM

The ringing began sooner this time, while Arthur was barely on Mountain View Drive. It was in the same ear, nagging and pestering. He moved his jaw, trying but failing to erase the sound.

"Are you okay?" Codi asked.

"Do you hear anything?"

She paused a moment. "No."

They turned onto Richlandtown Road and Arthur winced. He waved Codi off. "I'm okay."

"You're going to make your ear worse," she said. He did not answer.

The trees canopied the road the deeper they drove. The sun was at its highest, but it might as well have been dusk under the interwoven thicket. Arthur's ear was pulsing by the time they pulled up to the spot on the road where the shoulder of dirt pushed back just far enough to remind him that he was in the right place.

"This is it," he said over the ringing.

"Let me go first," Codi suggested.

He looked at her. "Absolutely not."

"Arthur, I feel fine. Look at you. You're in pain. Let me at least try."

"You're not going in there by yourself."

"And I don't want you hurting yourself any more." She reached for the door handle. "I said I wanted to help, right? Then let me help."

"Codi …"

She closed the door behind her and crossed in front of the vehicle. She traipsed through the initial blanket of leaves and weeds, leery of what lay beyond but moving swiftly nonetheless. The green on the ground was starting to wilt and die. A few patches of resilient flora held on strong, but it was only a matter of time. Arthur grunted, shut off the car, and got out.

The ringing amplified with his movement. He could still make out her figure as she pushed forward. The branches she shoved away snapped back in her face, but she ducked and swatted and thrashed, creating her own path. The leaves applauded and Codi looked behind her at Arthur making his way through. The car had all but disappeared from where they stood.

How far is this house? What if the thing has been bulldozed and overgrown? He looked up for the sun and then down at the trees. They needed a marker. Something to tell them where they'd come from, and, more importantly, how they could get back.

"Codi?" Arthur shouted as she pressed farther in, quicker than he was moving and becoming hard to see. "Can you hear me?"

"Yes. But these birds are loud."

"What birds?" he yelled back.

She halted. "You don't hear that?" she said as loudly as she could without screaming.

"I don't hear anything." The words seemed to come from in front of her. She spun around. "Arthur?"

He watched her turn in circles in the distance, nearly inaudible now. Eventually, she stumbled off to where he could no longer see her. He felt like he were moving in quicksand, his ear hurting something fierce.

12:09 PM

"Arthur," she shouted. "Arthur, can you hear me?"

"Yeah?" It came from her left. The birds chirped

louder.

"Yeah?" Now it was behind her.

"Yeah?" To her right.

"Yeah?" From every direction.

"Arthur!"

"Yeah?"

"Arthur, where are you!" She turned in a circle trying to find her bearings. "I can't …" Stay calm, she thought. Relax. She shut her eyes, trying to listen to the voice. There was a rustling in the leaves behind her. She jumped and let out a cry. "Arthur? Arthur, is that you?"

12:10 PM

He heard Codi scream and picked up speed, the ringing turning into a buzzing screech. "Codi, can you hear me?"

"Yes," she responded, but it came from behind him, in the direction of the car. He looked back over his shoulder and saw her leaning against a tree, facing the opposite direction. "I'm here, Arthur." It came from behind him again, in the direction of the house. He glanced back into the woods. Nothing. When he looked back to the tree, there was no one there.

12:10 PM

"Codi, can you hear me?"

Had to be him this time, she thought. It came from directly behind her. A sudden burst of adrenaline coursed through her body, and she darted ahead, deeper into the woods and towards the house.

12:12 PM

A scream echoed through the air, separate from the horrible sound in Arthur's head. He sprinted toward the noise, hurdling past fallen branches and pushing through scraping brush. "Codi? Goddammit, Codi, where are you?" The buzzing vibrated his brain and he stumbled face-first into a pile of leaves. "Codi?" he shouted again before standing up.

"Arthur?" She was closer.

Each step forward was more painful than the last and he fought to push on. Then he saw her. She was facing the opposite direction, standing still and peering around, trying to find her bearings. "Codi. Is that you?"

She turned and raced to him. "Your nose is bleeding," she said, grabbing his arm. "Let's get the hell out of here."

"Mama?" A familiar voice called out from behind the both of them. Codi refused to turn.

Arthur strengthened his legs as they both made their way closer to the road. A scream shook the trees. It was a scream of agony and torment. And frustration. It made the hair on his neck stand on end. "Run ahead," he said. "I'm okay."

"No."

"Codi! Goddammit, go!"

"No." She grabbed his arm again. "Keep moving."

The car appeared through the trees. It felt close enough to touch.

"Is it trying keep us here or scare us out?" Codi asked.

"Both," Arthur said, loud over the ringing. He groaned in pain. "I don't think it knows what the fuck it wants."

Something snagged Codi's foot. She wrangled it free, her shoe coming off in the process. She left it behind. The dirt had just about turned into road under their feet when Arthur took a glance at the evergreens to their right. What looked like a figure ran through the trees and out of sight. He turned back and tore open his car door, urging Codi through first. She climbed across the center console and into her seat. He hopped in behind her and shut the door. For a brief moment, there was nothing but the sound of them gasping for air. Interrupting the quiet of the car was the cry of what seemed like dozens of voices. Arthur threw his shifter into gear and sped away.

9.

Sunday, October 11, 2015, 3:07 PM

The hot cloth melted the dried blood from his face. He snapped his fingers a few times to make sure the hearing had returned to his right ear. It had, but not without a small muffling.

"I think you should go back to the hospital."

"No," he said. "No more hospitals. I just want to sit." He brushed off his jeans and tugged at the fresh hole in the knee. He pulled it open and found a superficial scrape on the skin just below the kneecap.

Codi hovered next to him, wringing the red-tinged washcloth into the sink. She was limping around his front when he noticed spots of crimson on her sock.

"Sit," he instructed.

"Let me just ..." she started, rubbing at the remaining spots on his face. She tossed the rag in the sink and sat next to him at the kitchen table.

He reached down and lifted her leg onto his lap and removed her sock. On top of her foot was a cut that ran from just above the webbing of her first and second toe to her ankle. It started deep and trailed off to barely more than a scratch. At its deepest, he could see the skin opening and closing as he moved it. Fresh blood pooled. She started at the pain, yanking her foot back. Arthur got up and retrieved rubbing alcohol from the bathroom. He grabbed gauze and medical tape too, both from the first aid kit he kept under the sink.

"Grab my arm," he said, pulling his chair closer to hers using one arm. He propped her leg across his lap and used the same washcloth to wipe the blood away from the cut. Then, he unscrewed the cap from the alcohol bottle. "Squeeze," he said, and poured a stream of liquid onto the cut. She trembled and dug her fingers into his arm as the alcohol trickled off her foot and splashed onto the kitchen floor. Her fingernails, trimmed short, dug through the fabric of his sweatshirt. "One more." He wiped again, cleaning the area thoroughly. He took the gauze out of the box and placed it over the cut. She eased her grip on his shoulder, and he unrolled the dressing, wrapping it around her foot. He repeated this until he finished the roll, and then secured it with two pieces of medical tape. "Are you okay?"

She nodded, rotating her foot at the ankle. "Thank you."

"Listen to me," he said, placing his hand on her

shin. "I think it's time you take a step back."

She shook her head.

"I need you to understand. There is *no* reason for both of us to go through this. You need to be home with Cara."

Hurt and shame found its way onto her face.

"I know you think this is your fault. This is not your fault, my fault, or anyone else's fault. It wants us to think that, but it's not. It never was. We didn't have a choice, Codi. You didn't. I don't. It fucked you and it fucked me the moment our paths crossed. And now we're fighting it and it doesn't want that. We hit a nerve today. I hit it last week. We are hurting it by being there. John hurt it by being there. And it wants us to stay away. Maybe it doesn't want us to think that, but it does. And it's hurting us in return."

"I care about you," she said, pulling back some of the curls that had freed themselves from her ponytail.

"And I care about you," he said, moving the rest of the stray hairs away from her face. "Which is why you're going home and staying there."

She folded her hands in her lap. "I wonder if this happens to everyone who tries to fight back, if anyone has even gotten this close."

"John did. He tasted it. He saw something big while he was in that house. He relived something he can't remember. Those journals have the answers. They know where he went and what happened while he was there. They're still there. I know they are. And I'm going to get them."

"I can't sit back and watch," she said, carefully planting her foot on the floor and putting weight on it. She winced as she stood.

"It's not going to go on much longer," said Arthur. "It can't."

Tuesday, October 13, 2015, 12:38 PM

Simon dropped the pizza crust onto the plate. "Done," he announced, rubbing his stomach. "That was good. You enjoy it, bud?"

Edwin's eyes opened wide as he bit into another slice, making sure to grab a piece of pepperoni with his teeth. It broke free from the now room temperature cheese as he pulled it into his mouth with the rest of the bite. "Mmhmm."

Simon slid the can of coke over to him. "Finish it. I can't fit anything else."

"That's because you ate five slices, Dad!" Edwin said, still chewing, his mouth partially open. He washed it down with the coke.

"Don't tell your mother how much I ate," Simon said. "I'll get a text message asking me to go on a diet." They both chuckled. Edwin was still just a boy at eleven years old, but he was old enough to know the truth when he heard it. Simon did an admirable job of abstaining from bad-mouthing his ex-wife, Melinda, but sometimes a spade is a spade and it's hard not to say anything.

Melinda griped about Simon any chance she had. When his son was younger, Simon worried about the impact it might have on their relationship, but as the boy aged, Simon started to understand that the child would see for himself. Simon was certainly not free of guilt, either, and would face that music soon enough, too.

They had never been closer, even though Simon wished he got to see Edwin more. But he still picked him up from school and practices, got him every other weekend, and even some days in between. Today was one of those days.

"I love when you have days off school," Simon said.

"Me too!" That went without saying.

"How was practice yesterday? I think it's neat your town does fall baseball."

"Good," said Edwin. "Alan hit Perry in the face with a bat."

Simon looked up from his wallet. "What!"

"It was an accident. Perry had his catcher's mask on and all, but he was too close and when Alan swung, he hit him on the top of the mask and pulled it down. He had a cut on his forehead. It bled a lot."

"Was he okay? Did he need stitches?"

"Four." Edwin took another big mouthful of pizza. The kid could eat. He was Simon's son, no doubt, standing almost five-foot-three already. He was lanky, but would assuredly fill out as his teens came around.

"That's why I always tell you to make sure your helmet is on right and you're wearing your cup," Simon said. "You never know. Freak things happen all the time. One second you're fine, the next you're not."

"I know, Dad. The umps make us knock our cups before each game. Last week, Truman wasn't wearing his and had to knock on his nuts. He tried to make it sound like a cup, but it didn't and he couldn't play."

"Testicles."

Edwin scrunched his face.

"Testicles. Not nuts."

"They're called nuts, too, Dad. Or balls."

"Yeah, but …"

Simon's cell phone rang.

3:10 PM

Arthur paced his living room. "Come on … pick up."

On the third ring, Simon did. *"Hello?"*

"Simon, it's Arthur."

"What's up, man?"

No mincing words. "I'm ninety-nine percent sure I know where May is."

Arthur could hear Simon shushing his son in the background. *"You what? You're going to need to call the detectives, Arthur. Call them and then call me right back."*

Arthur shook his head even though Simon

couldn't see. "I can't do that."

"What do you mean?"

"I need your help."

"Arthur, if you know something, you need to get that information into their hands right away."

"It's nothing they can use," he said, running his fingers up and down the window blinds. Tiny puffs of dust spat from each one. "Can you meet me at the Pig tonight?"

"I can't risk my job."

"I would never ask you to. You just have to trust me. I know that's a stretch, but I promise it'll make sense after I tell you. Just give me ten minutes." Arthur waited for the rejection. He knew it had been a long shot, but Simon was his best chance at getting his hands on those journals.

"I'll meet you there at eight."

Arthur emptied his lungs.

"But Arthur, I swear to you that you're going to regret it if you're pulling something stupid." It was not a threat as much as a warning. For both of their sakes.

They hung up, and Arthur typed a text to Codi. *"I need you one last time. One LAST time."* He needed her no matter what, he thought.

"What do you need?" she responded.

"Can you get out tonight?"

"Yes."

"Meet me at my house at 7:30?"

7:48 PM

"Your parents are saints," Arthur said, holding the binder in one arm as he and Codi walked along West Bridge Street. Halloween decorations were our in abundance, with pumpkins sitting on the front stoops of just about every home and business. Skeletons and witches peered from windows and from behind trees. Strings of orange lights were draped over gates and doorways.

"They are. They love Cara so much. I'm blessed. They were like this before, but now they're just so thrilled to have her. I tell them I'm going out with friends, and they think I'm letting loose." She laughed. "Letting loose all right."

"I'm sorry I asked you out here tonight," he said. "I know I told you I didn't want you involved anymore, but you'll be making my life a lot easier. It won't take long to tell your side of it."

"I just let you babble on last night." She beamed up at him.

"Have you seen my wife at all?"

"No." The smile melted away, and she stared into the distance. "I rarely did before. Now I just make sure to assess the lobby and parking lot before walking. There is no reason for us to run into each other. I'm sure she's done her diligence to stay away from me as well. Have you spoken with her?"

"We got into a screaming match on the phone a few days ago. So, no, we haven't spoken. But we've yelled!"

"Sucks. Maybe it'll be different when May's back, you know? Maybe it's just a speed bump. I hope you two can work it out."

He didn't know if he hoped for the same thing. "How's your foot?"

She kicked it out ahead of her. "Sore on the top, but I can walk without a problem. Obviously. Otherwise I would have been dragging my leg behind me, wouldn't I?"

"Apt time of year."

"What about you? Your head?"

"I didn't slam my face into anything last night, so that's a plus." They veered right at the fork and onto Ferry Street. "My hearing is still muffled, though."

"The bruise looks better," she said, scoping the side of his face. The spectrum of colors had faded but was still prominent.

"It's weird. I don't think I've ever felt more alive." He played with the words in his head before saying them out loud. "I feel … everything, and I don't think I've ever really *felt* like this. It's like every pore in my body is wide open. It's not … it's not good or bad. It's just different."

They found themselves walking in the street. "Maybe instinct?" she said. "Fight or flight and all that. God, there were times I wanted to turn and run. I didn't *want* to handle it anymore. Especially before I had a clue about any of this." She waved at the binder lazily. "In a way, it was such a blessing. I can't imagine what I would be doing if I hadn't gone to see John."

"Probably finding out from someone else," he said. "I don't think it's possible to be ignorant to it. This is just how it is. If we'd never met John, it would've been someone else. Hell, look at the binder you filled from top to bottom without his help. That's either really intuitive, which, hey, you might just be." He held up his hands. "Or it's something else. Some contributing force. Either way, we're both here. That has to account for something. Would be some real coincidental shit if it were happenstance, huh?"

She nodded.

"I know if it weren't for you, I wouldn't … you know."

"You wouldn't be dealing with any of this," she said.

"That's not what I was going to say." He stopped walking and looked at her.

"I know it's not," she said, stopping too. "But it's the truth."

"Maybe it was for the best. Maybe we end this here and now."

"Meant to be." The sarcasm was thick.

"Yeah, I don't know about all that. Not really my cup of tea, either. But I think people who can't handle things wilt and die. Those who *can* handle it prosper. It's that way with anything, isn't it? Survival of the fittest. We're here because we're surviving." Each streetlight created a spotlight on the tar, and Arthur and Codi moved in and out of them as they walked.

"What did you do before all of this?"

She shrugged. "Worked. Dealt with my shitty boyfriend. Contemplated going back to school. Went out with friends whenever I could, which was almost never. It wasn't always like that, but having a child changes a lot."

"Exactly. How many people can say they're built for something like this? You don't know until you know. I was drawing on skin and paying a mortgage. My daughter changed my life in so many ways. But even with drastic changes, we tend to sleep through most things. Do you still sleep through your life?"

"No. Everything is different. Every day. Since the moment she disappeared." Codi kicked a pebble. It skipped on the street until it hit a car tire.

Arthur held his hands behind his back as he walked. "What gets me through, what helps me sleep, is thinking about that feeling. Experiencing life, wide awake, like I am right now. I know when I have her back, nothing will be the way it was."

"*When.*" Codi placed her own hands behind her back. "No, it won't be. But nothing ever stays the same."

They walked in silence the rest of the way to the restaurant.

8:25 PM

Simon sat back and shook his head. The binder

was open flat in front of him, the pages all to his left.

Arthur sat with his hands clasped in front of his mouth. "Nothing made sense. No fingerprints. No forced entry or exit." He rested back on the chair. "And I know you're privy to all the crazy shit that has gone on long before May. You said it yourself – you've heard the stories."

Simon crossed his arms, his face in a frown. The three of them were stationed in the back corner of the restaurant, Arthur and Codi with their backs to the room. All three had a beer on the table. Not one had taken a sip. "If you don't believe me, believe her." Arthur pointed his thumb at Codi. "You read her story. She told it to you. For Christ's sake, she's got her kid back. She's got quite literally no reason to lie to you. Why would she? Why would I? This is my kid's life."

Simon sat up and spoke low, looking around. "Have you ever thought that you might have lost your shit, Arthur? You're vulnerable and you have this one here feeding you all this."

"Excuse me?" Codi snapped.

Arthur held up a hand. "I haven't lost my mind. And she's not feeding me anything I can't see directly in front of my face, on those pieces of paper or from what I've witnessed myself. I went to her. She didn't come to me." Arthur put both hands on the table. The light from above accentuated the bags under his eyes and the healing bruise that made up most of one side of his face. "How long do we go back? Years.

We've known each other some time, Simon."

"And something like this will make you believe things you never thought possible," said Simon. "I've seen people do some ridiculous shit, Arthur. A glimmer of hope and you start grasping at straws. Maybe you just need some time to clear your mind, away from everything."

Codi glared at Simon from her seat.

"Look, I'm not saying you're a liar," he said to her. "But I-"

"You listen to me," Codi interrupted. "There was nobody in the whole world more screwed up than me. It's something you cannot imagine, and it's something I hope you never have to deal with. But to lie about my daughter? That's insulting. The only reason I have my daughter back is because I took things into my own hands. You, nor any of your colleagues, would have ever brought her home. I did. *Me.* And I don't need to sit here and take shit from you, not after what I've been through and where I've come from." She took a breath and evened her voice. "You need to listen to Arthur. You need to trust us. I'm sitting here telling you, a police officer, that *I'm* responsible for his daughter missing. Do you think for a minute that if I had any reservations about what we are both telling you that I would go along with this? I'm putting my daughter's life on the line again. After all she's been through, to risk her losing her mother to prison for who knows how long? Forever? I owe this to Arthur for doing what I did. Or what my ex-boyfriend did. Or what the person before him did. And I owe it to myself, so that I can atone for it and live a life *somewhat* guilt-free."

Arthur admired her from the side. "Simon," he said, moving the officer's attention. "I need your help. I need you to take my word for it. It's a leap. It's a leap, but you're the only person I can think of who can help. I don't really have anywhere else to turn right now."

"Does Sarah know about any of this?" Simon asked.

Arthur shook his head. "No. I've misled her for the last few weeks. Kept her in the dark. There was just no way. I wanted to," he said, playing with the wedding ring on his finger, "but I couldn't."

Pete looked their way from behind the bar, nodding his head, checking in. Simon shook him off.

"I've told you everything, Simon. You know it all. I'll be forever indebted to you if you do this."

Simon sniffed. "And all you want me to do is get into the house, get the journals, and we're out of there?"

"That's it," Arthur said. "If I could do it, I wouldn't drag anyone else into this, believe that."

Simon tapped his finger on the table.

"I can prove it to you if you just have a little faith in what I'm saying." said Arthur. "You can do whatever you need to do to make yourself comfortable." He reached into his back pocket and tossed his wallet onto the table, followed by his cell phone. "It's Vance State Park, over by Crux."

"I used to take my kid there when he was younger," said Simon.

"Then you know where it is. I'll give you my keys. You know my address. You know where my family lives. My wife's address. You can pat me down, carry your gun, whatever you want. We'll take your car." He held up his hands, surrendering. "I really need your help."

Simon drank half the pint in a few gulps. "Okay."

Arthur didn't expect it.

"I better get a tattoo out of this," Simon said, as he ran his hand along the stubble under his chin. It produced a grating sound.

"I don't even know how to say thank you."

"When do we leave?" Simon asked.

"Tonight. Right now." Arthur waited for a response. "Can we do it now?"

Simon tossed Arthur's wallet back to him. "It's for the better. I'll change my mind if we don't." He stood and Arthur waved him off, taking his wallet and walking over to Pete. He returned after settling the bill and the three made for the door. Simon handed the binder to Arthur who handed it to Codi. Arthur filled his lungs and stared at her.

"No," she said. "You're out of your goddamned mind if you think I'm not going."

"Go be with Cara," he said. "She needs you."

She dropped her shoulders. "You'll have to physically stop me from coming."

"Don't do this, Codi. Please. You remember what happened yesterday."

She wasn't budging. She looked at Simon. "I'll be the lookout. I'll keep an eye on the road."

"There won't be anyone out there," Arthur said.

"Just in case," she responded.

"That won't be an issue," said Simon, his hand moving to his hip. His biceps stretched his thermal shirt.

"There are some things you just can't shoot, Officer Shelley."

He cracked a smile, unconvinced.

"You're doing Arthur a favor, I get it," she said. "You might not believe any of this, but that's not going to stop it." She turned her attention to Arthur. "Three is better than two."

"You're not going to give up, are you?" Arthur asked, realizing they were standing in the middle of the restaurant doorway. "Fine," he said, opening the door for her. "Last time."

Simon trailed behind, his mind elsewhere, contemplating the insanity of what he was about to do.

Arthur waved to Pete, who was mid-conversation with someone at the other end of the bar. Greg, he realized.

8:41 PM

Codi sat in the passenger seat of the SUV, Arthur behind her in the backseat. All had been quiet until Simon turned onto 223.

"So how are we approaching this?" Simon asked quietly, directing his voice back toward Arthur. Arthur described the road, the clearing, and the supposed house, set back in the woods, and Simon gripped the wheel a little tighter. "So, all of this mind game stuff you were talking about ..."

"It prevents people from getting close," said Arthur. "It gets violent with me, tries to confuse me. For Codi, it screwed with her head too. For John Braun, it was the same as Codi. He was shocked to see how physical it got with me. He had never seen that before, of all the times he's sent people in, so he says."

"And how big of a club is that?"

"I don't know. I never asked." Arthur played with the window button, accidentally opening it a crack. The sudden sound of the road ripping by outside startled Codi and she flinched. Arthur closed it again.

"It knows when you're there for it," Codi said, turning to Simon.

"It protects something," said Arthur. "And that's what we want. That something. And I think those journals will lead us to whatever it is."

"Do you think that's why John was chased away?" asked Codi.

"Of course," Arthur said, moving the window a second time. He closed it again and put his hands in his lap. "I don't understand why it didn't happen to him from the beginning, though. It took a while before fucking with him. Maybe it was because John meant no harm and was none-the-wiser at first. Or maybe it was because it didn't expect John to see what he saw. And once he wrote it down, it knew it could be exposed. Or even exorcised somehow. I don't know, maybe that's why it took so long for him to get out of there. As he got closer to figuring things out, it became aware. There's an incredible energy there."

Simon accelerated.

"And maybe it doesn't control itself one hundred percent. This residual *whatever* that comes off of it is just there waiting to be heard or seen. Energy, I guess. And so it convolutes people with confusion and visions and voices and whatever else. And for whatever reason, the deeper into the woods you go – maybe even the closer to that house, that land – the worse it is. It's *the* nerve, it seems. And it protects that."

"Why worse for you?" Simon asked. Arthur sensed concession in the cop's voice – *I don't believe it completely, but I'm here, and I might as well try to understand where you're coming from.*

Arthur shrugged, alone in the backseat.

"Because he's intuitive," said Codi. "He's all over it. Has been from day one. He believes it, and knows it's true." The cars thinned the closer they came to the park.

"I don't know about that," said Arthur. "I didn't believe it entirely right away. Even when I said I did, it wasn't wholly the truth. It was more like I adopted it."

"Whatever it was," Codi said, "you're just as interested in stopping it as you are in getting your daughter back. And I think it's threatened."

The car fell silent again.

Simon finally said, "When I show up to arrest someone who's stolen something, I'm not there to take it back and return it to its owner. I'm there to take care of the person responsible. And when that person is desperate, what do they do? They lie, they run, they get violent. They'll try to punch us, stab us, shoot us. Anything not to be stopped. Desperation."

"Hopefully it doesn't have much more to throw at us," said Arthur. He rubbed his forehead, thinking about what Simon had said. The ache had all but gone. "Turn right at the next road."

"And me?" Simon asked. "How do you think this, *whatever*, is going to affect me?" The tone was slightly condescending, but Arthur ignored it.

"I'm hoping not at all," said Arthur. "I'm hoping we're taking it by surprise. Realistically, I just don't know. What I do know is that I don't expect you to put yourself in a position to get hurt. That's not why I asked you to come out here. I just want to see if it affects you the same way. If at all. You're not involved. You have no dog in the fight, not that it knows of, anyway. Maybe you can sneak on by. Get what we need and get out, you know?"

"And if I can't?"

"We leave. We turn around and go home."

Simon looked at him in the rearview.

"We only do this if you promise to leave if and when I say. No heroes. No police officer shit. Just a friend doing a favor. Cool?"

Simon agreed.

"Hang a left here. Then the first right. It comes up quick." Arthur leaned against the turns. "We're going to pass another road. Then there's a clearing, where the shoulder on our left gives way. Just slow up and we'll see it." A low ringing pierced his right ear.

It knows we're here, he thought.

"How do we do this in the dark?" Codi asked.

"You're going to stay in the car, in the driver's seat. The car stays on, windows up, locked. I'm going to get out with Arthur."

She agreed.

"I want him to walk up a few steps," Arthur said. "See how he feels. If he's okay with it, he can go farther in. I'm going to follow for as long as I can."

"Arthur-" she started.

"I'm okay," he interrupted, resting a hand on Codi's on the center console. "Here," he said, pointing to the side of the road. "Spin the truck around so we can get back in quickly if we need to."

Simon put the truck into park and fumbled for

something next to Codi's legs on the passenger side, finally pulling it free. A Maglite. He handed it back to Arthur, who clicked it on and off. Simon pulled his own Maglite from the same place.

Arthur inhaled and held it for a second, working up the courage to open the door. He closed his eyes and thought of May. Where was she right now? Was she aware? Was she afraid? The simmering of nerves turned to boiling anger and the butterflies were gone as quickly as they'd come. He put his hand on the handle but paused. "If you hear cries, it's not May."

Simon paused.

"If something calls your name from somewhere else, it's not human. If you're susceptible, it will try to lure you deeper into the woods. It will try to confuse you to no end and anything else it can do to throw you off. If that happens, turn around and walk out. *Don't* fight it."

"We'll be good to go," said Simon. "I'm okay."

"Let's hope it stays that way."

Simon and Arthur closed the doors behind them, and Codi hopped into the driver's seat. She shifted into drive and held the brake, ready.

"Thank you for doing this," Arthur said once outside the truck, extending a trembling hand. Simon shook it. "I owe you. Sliders. Beer. Whatever." The ringing intensified.

"A tattoo," Simon said, smirking.

"Deal."

The moon was new on this clear night. A gentle

but steady breeze circulated, not freezing but cold nonetheless. Simon turned and stepped over the initial brush while clicking on the flashlight and aiming it ahead of him.

"Anything weird? Are you hearing noises?"

"Just you," Simon said, laughing and edging closer to the trees. He disappeared after a few more steps, his light the only thing visible.

He still doesn't buy it, Arthur thought, looking back to Codi. "Stay here. Please." He spun around and the movement hurt his ear, stabbing deep inside. He ignored it and followed the flashlight in front of him, keeping distance between Simon and himself. He peered back frequently, watching the headlights. *We should've done this at night all along.* Following the light was much easier than following the sound of a voice. He clicked on his light now, aiming it mostly at the ground as he trudged through.

10.

Tuesday, October 13, 2015, 9:29 PM

Codi fiddled with the button on the emergency break handle, pushing it in and out. Her stomach grumbled, a mix of hunger and nerves.

The lights dawdled back and forth as the two men made their way through the woods, Arthur's slightly brighter and larger than Simon's, both slowly shrinking in size and luminosity the deeper they traveled.

She wanted to get out of the car and follow them in. *They need me here*, she repeated to herself, but other thoughts flittered in and out of her head. *But why would we need a quick getaway?*

Pain.

The word resonated as a third light flickered on deep in the woods, quite a distance from the other two.

What the hell is that? Shit. Cops. They followed us in.

That's okay, Simon's there.

By the time the words came to mind, the light went off. She lowered the window and listened. Both Arthur and Simon's lights frantically searched around them. Then, at the same time, both of their lights went off, and it was pitch black in the forest. She gasped and waited for them to turn back on. Five seconds. Ten. Nothing. She listened but could not hear much over her rapid breathing, so she held it in. What sounded like the plucking of banjo strings startled her. Frogs, she realized. *In this cold weather?* Not cold enough, perhaps. They would stay high in the water or on the land until it got too cold. She remembered that from when she was a child and they kept her awake at night. "It'll stop soon," her father told her. "Even they don't like the cold. They hibernate too. Just like the bears!" Damn things were annoying her now just as much as they did then.

"Shut. Up." She whispered the words and leaned forward, searching the noise for anything resembling a voice. Nothing. A light breeze tossed some leaves around the truck. Nothing, again. Until ... something ... no, not a voice. A humming. Another car? A plane. It soared in the distance, rumbling to another moment of silence. She concentrated hard, honing in on anything she could when, all at once, dozens of flashlights, of all different depths and strengths, flashed on at precisely the same time.

Codi yelped and jumped backwards in her seat.

None of the lights moved. All were still,

encompassing the woods from left to right, as far as she could see. She gasped for air, realizing she was still holding her breath. Her heart rate spiked to an unhealthy level and sobs built in her throat, stuck, as the fear prevented her from making a sound. She squeezed the emergency brake handle as her legs turned to rubber and tingled.

Then the lights went off.

9:32 PM

"Simon," Arthur whispered. "Can you hear me?" He had been able to keep up to an extent, but the ringing amplified every few feet, close to screeching now. His left ear was clear, and he led with that side of his head cocked in front of him. "Simon, I can't go much more. Just look for the house." The light in front of him stopped. He heard footsteps as Simon backtracked toward him.

"How much farther up is it?" Simon asked.

"I'm not sure. Another hundred-fifty yards, maybe? Are you okay?"

"I'm fine," he said. "You look like shit. You okay?"

"It's my ear."

"Your face looks fucking horrible," said Simon. "The bruise ... it's awful."

Arthur felt the skin on his forehead and grimaced. It was sore, as sore as when he first hurt it. "It was fine a minute ago."

"Did you hit it on a branch?"

Arthur shook his head. "It's fucking with us."

"Huh?"

"It's fucking with us. My face is fine." He felt the skin again; it was normal. He looked around. "We should go."

Simon cocked his head. "Why?"

"Because it's got you too." He sneered into the darkness, frustrated. "Fuck!"

Simon frowned. "I'm fine."

"Remember what I told you in the car."

"I'm going to go a little more," he said. "Don't sweat it." There was an apprehension in his voice that hadn't been there before, but Arthur could tell he was ignoring it.

There was a shuffling in the distance and both men froze. Simon held up his hand and turned off his flashlight. He motioned for Arthur to do the same. They sat in silence, waiting for the noise again, but it never came and they both put their lights back on.

"Deer," said Simon, and forged ahead.

Arthur hesitated. "I'll catch up." The ringing had become deafening, so loud and painful that his right eye started to tear. He wiped it away and leaned against a tree, keeping his flashlight aimed ahead, sweeping the area constantly. Simon was still visible, though the cracks and pops of his footsteps dissipated in the night and in Arthur's muffled hearing.

From his peripheral, Arthur caught sight of movement. It was a blur, but discernably different from anything he would expect in the empty wood. He trained his eye to the general vicinity, widening his lids and staring intently where his light illuminated. Was that him breathing so hard? No. It was not breathing at all. It was something sliding. Something dragging. Along the dead leaves and hardened grass behind him.

Phhhtt. Phhhhttt.

He jerked around and flashed the light on anything he could find.

"*Simon*," he whispered, though it came out more like a growl. "*Simon*."

The dragging persisted. It was coming toward him, more pronounced with each effort. He could feel his heart. Or was he hearing it?

"It's only in your mind," he said to himself.

Phhhhhhhttttt.

9:34 PM

Simon searched the immediate area. It seemed even darker than it had been only a few steps back. More trees, he thought. He flashed a look behind him. *Must've turned his light off,* he thought. *He's staying put. I'll flash my light at him when I'm on my way back.*

Simon moved in a straight line, or so he hoped. Overshooting the house by being off-course would be a real pain in the ass. Could even get him stuck out here until morning, he mused while whacking away stray branches and brush with his arm, climbing over what he could not move.

Something with wings buzzed in his ear and he jumped hard to the left, waving his hand and dropping his flashlight. "Goddammit." It was buried in a pile of dank leaves and vegetation. The light was smothered. He crouched to pick it up, bending at the knees, when something rammed his shoulder, knocking him sideways into the pile. At once, he rolled to his back and pulled the pistol from his waist, aiming it at the air in front of him. "I've got a weapon," he shouted. "I will fire." He could see nothing and moved his aim back and forth in the darkness, eventually removing a hand from the gun and reaching into the slush next to him, fishing out the flashlight. He braced the gun across his opposite wrist and aimed the light ahead. Nothing there.

He stood, slowly, still searching. In one motion, something slapped the gun. It flew easily from his grasp, sailing a few feet away. He pointed his light frantically around his body.

9:34 PM

"Simon?" Arthur asked. "Simon, is that you?" He gritted his teeth and pushed his body forward, leaving the sliding sound behind, dragging whatever it was to wherever it intended. Away from him. Even if it was only in his mind.

"Simon, will you fucking answer me?" he said, no longer trying to conceal his voice. Perhaps he had answered and Arthur could not hear it through what was now the buzzing screech, just as bad as it was the last time. It nearly brought him to his knees, but he managed to keep upright and totter forward. Or what he hoped was forward.

Somewhere far, far away, a dog yapped. He wondered if the animal was listening to them traipsing around the empty woods, searching for an invisible house and yelling at invisible spooks. Its owner must have given it hell, because it stopped.

He'd planned on getting May a puppy when she was old enough to appreciate it.

A ball of light flashed on and off from up ahead. A burst of three, followed by three more. It continued. Simon. Finally. He clicked his flashlight in response. Nothing happened for a moment, but another three flashes came from Simon's direction. Arthur stiffened and walked ahead, his ear screeching.

9:36 PM

Codi's heart rate slowed – not quite normal, but better. *It's screwing with me,* she thought. No quicker than the thought raced through her mind, something shrieked from the woods, echoing into the cabin of the car. The hair on her arms stood on end as the goose bumps sprouted across her skin.

You're not luring me in.

Another scream. This time it sounded like two people. She fidgeted on the balls of her feet, wanting to spring from the car, but she knew better. She would not give in to these bastard woods. So she fought back tears, choking them away.

Strong.

A violent wind whipped through the area, sending leaves swirling into the air. Some drifted lightly down onto the hood and windshield of the car. More followed. She searched for the windshield wipers, but could not find the knob. Goddamn new cars and their million controls. More and more leaves blanketed the glass, leaving only small areas of black night between them. Eventually, every nook and cranny was filled by a solid mass of dead leaves. She exhaled through her tight lips as she finally found the knob on the blinker handle and spun it. When the wipers came to life and brushed everything away, the faces of dozens of children stared back at her, their mouths gaping wide, though nothing but the moaning of the wind could be heard. The shock stiffened her body and she shut her eyes. When she opened them, the faces were gone.

9:36 PM

Simon stood frozen, ready for another blow,

hesitant to bend for the gun now buried somewhere beneath him. The wind made it hard to detect anything other than the sounds immediately surrounding his body.

Focus.

A figure in the distance caught the edge of his light. He brought the beam back but could not find the shape again. After a tick, he heard footsteps. They edged closer.

"Simon?"

"Arthur?" he responded, whispering. He shined the light in front of him, but there was nothing there. A hand grabbed his shoulder and he yelled and spun around.

"Simon," Arthur said, "Jesus, it's me." He squinted through the brightness of the Maglite. Simon pulled him close, searching around the both of them. "Someone … some*thing's* here. It knocked me over, knocked my gun out of my hand. It's here somewhere," he said, swiveling his head every few seconds. "Where the hell were you just calling me from?"

"What?"

"My name. Where were you when you were just calling my name?"

"What are you talking about? I didn't call you," Arthur said, cupping his hand over his right ear. The pain was written all over his face. "I could see your light. I didn't want to shout. Some dog was barking like Cujo a second ago. I don't want to get busted out here."

"What dog?"

Arthur, still holding his ear, shook his head. "Fuck."

"Someone called my name, before you got here."

"No, they didn't."

"Arthur, I'm telling you. It was barely louder than a whisper but clear as day."

"No one called your name. There was no dog. No one knocked you over." His voice grew with each word. He could not hear how loud he was as he tried to speak over the sound in his head. "It's got to be right here somewhere. It's getting worse."

Simon pulled his face back from the volume of Arthur's voice. "I don't know, maybe you were right," he said. "This is fucking me up."

"Then let's get the hell out of here."

"No," said Simon. "We can't be far, can we?"

"I don't know. I don't think so." A sharp pain sliced through his ear canal and into his head. He jerked his neck and his eye started to water again. He wiped it with his free hand. "But who the fuck knows?"

"Go back," Simon said.

"Good, let's go."

"No, you go." He spoke up and into Arthur's better ear. "I'll meet you out there. Give me five more minutes." Simon held up five fingers in front of Arthur's face. "If I can't find it, we'll come back during the day."

Arthur was willing to say anything to get him out of the woods. "I'll only come back with you if you leave with me now."

"*Dada.*" The voice came from behind Arthur. "*Dada.*" He pinched his eyes shut. "Now Simon!"

"Five minutes. Give me five minutes."

"*Dada!*" It was a screech, and it ripped through his good ear now, a burning tear that made him cry out loud. Everything went silent. "Shut up!" he yelled back.

Simon felt around with his shoes until he kicked the gun. He scooped it up without taking his eyes off Arthur. "Five minutes," he said one more time before turning and jogging deeper into the woods.

Arthur did not hear a word, but swallowed hard when Simon took off. "Stop," he said, half-heartedly. He couldn't even hear himself.

9:38 PM

Simon dipped below a branch. "There's no one out here," he told himself. "Fucking idiot. Middle of the woods on a weeknight in West Bumblefuck, Pennsylvania. Even the psychos and cultists wouldn't be out here now." He stumbled over something and caught himself before face-planting. "The hell was that? Why the hell is there a cinderblock out-" He looked to his right and raised the flashlight. A small cabin, no bigger than a two-car garage, stood in a small clearing of mostly dirt. The patch of land was about the size of a baseball infield, bordered on one side by overgrown bushes and a small, makeshift rock wall. Grass was few and far between, mostly in front of the house itself, sprawling up the rotting planks of wood, of which some were missing completely. The square windows were both intact, with the front door constructed between them. There had been a porch with an overhang, but the supports were long toppled and the wood was hanging on for dear life. The door was closed but with no latch or locking mechanism to speak of, and no "No Trespassing" signs of any sort. If the city or state knew this shitty structure existed, it had not done a very thorough job keeping anyone out. *They've forgotten all about it*, he thought, keeping his gun in front of him.

He turned in a circle, feeling more comfortable with the open land around him. Nowhere to hide.

If I get killed here, what the hell would they think I was doing? Looking for drugs? He laughed out loud. *No, no one in their right mind would be out here looking to score. So then what? I'm a cop. On a case? I'm not a detective. That wouldn't make sense either. I was lured out here for something. That's it. That's what they'd say. No ... my body was dumped here. Uh huh. Nothing else they'd come up with. I'm not even on duty. Though forensics would figure out I was alive here at one point. Maybe they brought me out here to kill me. I guess that all depends on how they do it. Maybe they'll bash my head in with that cinder block. That would be messy, but worth it. I bet the block would break before crushing my skull. I do have a gun. Maybe they take it and beat the shit out of me with it, then put a few in my head. Or in my body, then my head. Make me suffer a little while first. They might even force me to turn my own hand around and put the muzzle in my mouth, blowing my brains through the back of my skull. They'd find fragments of bone all over. Arthur would probably run once he heard the shot. Goddamn pussy. He's probably already gone. Him and his bitch. His little sidepiece. She's probably the reason his wife isn't around. Probably had his cock buried deep down her little throat. Of course he did. On his and his wife's bed. Abandoning her daughter after just getting her back. Little bitch didn't deserve the kid back in the first place. Should've left her for dea ..."*

He blinked and shook his head hard. *What the hell was that? God in heaven, what the hell was that? It's in my head*, he thought. *Nope. Not having that. Fuck off.*

Decayed and decrepit wood littered the way to the front door, so he holstered his gun and climbed the mess, aiming the light around him every few seconds, making sure he was still alone. He searched the perimeter of the fallen porch before pressing on the front door. When it refused to budge, he shoved harder. Nothing. Inspecting the gap between the flimsy wood and the doorframe, he found a latch and padlock on the inside. *How the hell did the person get out? Or are they still ...?* He drew his gun again.

"If there's anyone in there, I'm coming in. I'm Officer Simon Shelley of the New Hope, Pennsylvania Police Department and I am armed." He knocked a second time using the back end of the

Maglite and no one answered. *The window.* He shined the light inside. It took a few seconds to adjust his eyes away from the reflection in the dingy, gray-filmed glass. The room inside was small. A cot was positioned up against the back wall, foam stuffing spewing from the thin mattress like a leaky pudding cup. A desk adorned the side wall with an old throw rug underneath. He panned down onto the floor closest to him. There were piles of framed art and linens wrapped around each other. Garbage bags full of crap were piled in the corner. No signs of life in any of it, however. He returned to the door.

No one is going to give a shit if the door is open or closed. With that thought, he pulled back his leg and kicked the door as hard as he could. It exploded open, forcing the latch clean off the wood. The lock dangled on the end of it, anchored to the doorjamb. Simon took one more look around and entered the house.

9:41 PM

Arthur rested against a tree, his eyes closing for a moment. The allure of the woods had long worn off and even the hallucinatory voices and footsteps had lost their luster. They were fake. He knew that. He *knew* that before, but now he believed it. The near-deafness had subsided a small degree every time he took a rest, which was tree-to-tree at this point.

A clatter jerked him alert. It sounded as though a branch had snapped away from a tree, but there was no crash. Another hallucination. He leaned again onto the trunk and waited for Simon to return.

9:41 PM

Codi hugged herself. Her legs were pulled up onto the car seat, knees to her chest and her arms wrapped around them.

Not real, she thought. *Not real. None of it.* She rocked, tears streaming down her face and a chill shooting through her body, even though the heat was blasting. It was getting so cold, in fact, that the windows began to fog. She turned the dial to defrost and, while the windshield was clearing, she lowered and raised the rest of the windows, wiping away the fog. The truck was pulled as close to the edge of the road as possible, the right side no more than a few feet from the trees. It had been over twenty minutes since they'd left, and she wondered if they were okay. *Unless they found the house. They might be trying to find the books. Maybe they found them and are on their way back. I hope Arthur is okay. He could not have lasted this long the same way he was yesterday. Something had to give. He could be hanging back, playing relay for Simon.*

A man appeared in the distance, walking on the road in front of her. He was directly in line with the front of the car and moving in her direction.

Something was on his head, a hood, perhaps, but she could not tell from her vantage point. He walked with vigor, about an eighth of a mile away. What perturbed her was not the man himself, though she was certainly uncomfortable about someone walking around at this time of night in such a desolate area. But for all she knew, he lived down the road and was on a nightly walk. No, what made her uncomfortable was the gray sheen that seemed to encompass his entire body. His clothes, his skin, all of him, emanated a slight shine, as if he had just been spritzed with a bottle of water. It had not been raining and was forty-five degrees at most. No one would be comfortable walking around in a damp set of clothes, never mind hiking through the hilly roads and forests of Vance State Park. It was not normal. Not now. Not while they were here for this reason. This was something else. A mind game? Something messing with her? Whatever it was, he was gaining speed, determined in his approach.

She reached into her coat pocket and pulled out her keys. A small canister of pepper spray dangled from the chain, and she gripped it tight and slid the locking mechanism to the right, finding the trigger with the tip of her thumb. She held it ready as the man closed the distance between the two of them.

Shift the car into drive, she thought, and dropped the pepper spray onto the passenger seat. She depressed the brake and pulled the shifter into place.

There was a crash in the distance, and the man stopped in his tracks, flashing a look into the woods.

He turned and stared directly at her. It was not a hood but a mat of fabric. Or hair. His face was as gray as the rest of his body, and just as moist. His skin appeared scaly, though it may have been caked with mud. He reminded her of a shark, and that was only magnified when he smiled a wretched sneer, baring his bright white teeth. In an instant, he turned to his left and leapt into the darkness.

Arthur, she thought. She threw the car in park and ripped through the door, rounding the back of the truck and sprinting into the woods.

9:41 PM

Simon kicked at some debris on the cabin floor, and a cloud of dust and years of rot plumed back at him, swirling and dancing in the beam of light from his hand. He shuffled around some more, looking under old papers and on empty bookshelves. The mattress on the cot was only six inches thick and concave in places from where the stuffing had escaped through the torn fabric. Simon folded half of it over, exposing the metal support underneath, long rusted and warped. It was bare.

That just about did it in terms of possible hiding places, so he got to work looking in the place Arthur described, the floorboards in the middle of the room. He lowered his light and began stomping around, looking for any loose planks. He walked quickly over the entire area, stepping heavily. When nothing budged, he pressed on both ends of each plank using the heel of his boot. Finally, directly in the center, a little less secure than the rest and without nails holding it in place, a plank gave way. He worked it with his foot until it started to wobble and then jostled it free using both hands while the flashlight, pinned between his neck and shoulder, illuminated the area. It popped out of its slot and shot into the air, just missing his face, then clanked harmlessly to the floor. He wiggled the board next to it, and that too freed after a small fight. They had not been moved in decades, but once the first had been taken out, each consecutive one freed quicker than the one before it.

After removing five, Simon had a gap large enough to reach into. Hell, he could've hopped down through it if necessary.

No.

He peered down into the open space. It smelled of mold and mildew, the type of smell that ruined the soft pink of the lungs. He lowered his face down slowly, sweeping back and forth. Aside from a few spider webs and rotting hunks of wood, it was nothing but dirt, and the dirt was about two-and-a-half feet down. He felt around the loose earth. *If they're still around, they've got to be right here.*

He resurfaced into the cabin and examined the neighboring floorboards. Two more popped off with ease; the rest were held in place with nails, having been undisturbed for the better part of a century, if not longer. He now had the full width – about two feet. Back down he went, arms in, head beneath the surface.

He ran one hand along the dirt, shoving it from side to side, while trying to steady the light, looking for any signs of a box. The earth moved easily, and he began digging, tossing the dirt back and forth until a ditch formed. After six inches or so, he stopped and shifted about a foot to the right. Nothing. Back the other way he dug. Something shiny glared back at him. It was metal. He tapped on it with the tips of his fingers. It sounded hollow. Had to be a box. *Has to be it.*

Somewhere outside, someone screamed. He paused a moment, then continued digging. *I'm close, aren't I?*

9:45 PM

Arthur jerked his head upright. He was not even sure the scream was real. Perhaps he had nodded off.

9:45 PM

Codi stopped dead in her tracks, almost falling over. The *thing* was long gone from her sight, but the screech pierced her ears, throwing her equilibrium for a loop.

"Arthur!" she yelled. "Arthur, where are you!"

She took off running in the same direction.

9:46 PM

Simon dusted off the top of the metal container. Rust revealed itself along with patches of blue. A thin metal handle was attached in the center. The box was immense, spanning nearly the entire width of the hole. He dug some dirt from the front side, checking to see if the clips were buckled. They were, and he attempted to lift the entire thing from the aperture. The box was packed too tightly and the handle too skinny – it hurt the creases of his fingers. He dropped back into the room and pulled the sleeve of his sweatshirt lower, covering his hand. The new cushion gave him some support, and he pulled again. It budged, lifted an inch, and dropped back down into its nest. After a breath, Simon pulled again, this time with all his strength, and the tin slid up and out of the hole. After another rest, he pulled it all the way out and dropped it onto the wooden floor. It clattered, echoing around him.

He sat next to it and eyeballed the room again, checking the windows and open doorway. Still alone.

He unhooked the first buckle by lifting the latch and pulling the metal loop over the protruding hook. He did the same on the opposite side and pulled open the top. It bounced on its hinges.

9:48 PM

Codi navigated without light. She guessed at a direction and, even with some moonlight, she was shit out of luck if she took a wrong turn. The car's headlights had been long lost behind her.

What looked like an orb of light swaying back and forth, obfuscated at times by the many trees between her and whatever the light source was, caught her attention. Arthur, she hoped.

"Mama, why did you leave me home?"

The voice was uncanny. Without a doubt it was Cara. But the elocution was too advanced.

"You do a good impression," Codi said. "But not great."

"Mama, come home."

"You're not my daughter," she roared, louder with each word, gutturally, her teeth clenched.

"Mama, anything could be happening to me right now." The voice changed midway through. It morphed deep and tormented, almost whining. "Something could be crushing me by my little fucking throat."

Codi closed her eyes tightly. "You had your chance," she said. "You blew it."

9:49 PM

Arthur rocked his Maglite back and forth nervously as he waited. *He's taking too long. Something isn't right. I should go in after him. I should-*

"Codi?" he shouted. "Codi is that you?"

9:50 PM

"Present owner: Richard Porter," Simon read. "Former owner: Daniel Gilbert. Date of deed: May 12th, 1929." He glanced over the rest of the paper. "Look at that penmanship." He dropped it on top of a few other pieces of paper he'd pulled from the box.

Scattered inside the metal container were photographs of the house and the surrounding land. He picked them up and shuffled through. Some were more recent, standard four-by-six in size and in color. Others were square in shape, stamped with dates from the fifties and sixties. Two were possibly even older than that, likely from the purchase of the property. Other than the deteriorating condition and a blanket of snow on the ground, nothing about the house had ever changed. No additions, no renovations, no decorations. He placed the pictures on top of the pile he had created on the ground.

Back inside the box were the last remaining contents: six spiral notebooks. He pulled one out and paged through it. Script filled the journal cover to cover, in perfect penmanship.

"I can't close my eyes without seeing him," Simon read aloud. "He sits next to me at times, writing on a non-existent desk. He lived here, I'm sure of it. Though, possibly not in this very house. Rebuilt, likely. I feel as though I'm in his territory. Like I'm trespassing." Simon shook his head and closed the book. *This is them. Son of a bitch was right.*

He tossed everything back into the tin and closed it. "Time to get the fuck out-"The door slammed shut.

9:50 PM

Codi picked her way closer to the light, jogging through openings when they were there, making paths where there were none.

"Arthur?"

"Codi?" he answered loudly, seeing her through the trees. "What are you doing here?"

She stopped short when she saw his face. Both ears were trickling a stream of blood, the bruise on his forehead eggplant in color. His eyes were bloodshot and he was hunched over in pain.

"Arthur, Jesus," she wrapped her arms around him to keep him upright.

"I'm okay. Simon should be back any minute. He's been gone awhile. I'll bet he found them." He was delirious.

"It doesn't matter anymore. Let's just go."

He didn't respond.

"Arthur," she pulled back and looked at his face.

"Let's go."

The words came from her mouth but he couldn't hear a word aside from a low grumble.

"Can you hear me?"

He shook his head, reading her lips. "Not really. There's a lot of pressure."

She looked around. They would need to leave Simon behind, she concluded. From over her shoulder, Arthur noticed movement again. A person this time, but not Simon. Whoever it was charged through the woods, seemingly unaffected by the rogue branches and thorny plants. The person was wearing a gray jumpsuit, his hair in disarray and his stride long and determined. He blew by the two of them.

Simon.

Arthur pushed off of Codi and turned to follow the man, stumbling and falling to his hands. He felt the healing skin over his knuckles snap apart, followed by warmth rushing between his fingers. "Simon!" he yelled out. Codi bent over to help him to his feet.

"Stay here," he yelled, turning to look at her and stumbling ahead.

9:52 PM

Simon, gun drawn, edged toward the door, his hand reaching for the handle.

One.

All was quiet. The windows were clear through to the forest. No shadows, no noises.

Two.

He fixed his finger on the trigger.

Three.

The door flung open before he touched the handle, sending him reeling backwards. His boot caught the edge of a swollen board, and he fell over, knocking the box over onto its side where it popped open and spewed its contents all over the floor. Simon's elbow thudded heavily to the wood and the gun discharged as his finger reacted to the shock. The bullet blasted from the barrel, striking the corner of the tin box and ricocheting harmlessly into a wall. The muzzle flash sparked the dead grass and leaves on the dry, rotting wood, and an ember took hold, burning through the fibers. A wisp of smoke danced away from the small fire as it grew. Simon jerked his hand back into place, holding his weapon toward the open doorway.

9:53 PM

Arthur bumbled deeper into the woods, bare sticks whipping his cheeks and ears. He ignored the pain as best he could, but the pressure in his head was excruciating. What sounded like a Fourth of July popper exploded somewhere ahead of him.

9:53 PM

Gunshot. Oh, God. Oh, God. Simon shot someone. Or someone shot ... no. No.

Codi wanted to run. Which way, she didn't know, but standing still was impossible. *If I get to the car, I can go get help. But where? How? What if they come running out and I'm not here? How the hell do I even get back to the car?*

The light from Arthur's Maglite was shrinking by the second. Soon, she would have no choice *but* to stand still. So she took off after him.

9:55 PM

Flames licked up from the floorboard, which had practically ignited once the fire took hold of the kindling around it. It traveled from plank to plank quickly.

Simon scrambled to his feet and tore towards the door, his gun ahead of him. Whoever, whatever, was outside of that door would need to react quickly, because he was ready to shoot the hell out of it. No more cat and mouse.

He maneuvered deftly through the threshold, inadvertently kicking one of the notebooks out the door. He searched around and his elbow throbbed with every movement, but the area was clear. He relaxed.

"The fuck is with this place," he said, looking up to the roof. He stepped down onto the grass and remembered the box inside. By now, the fire had spread through the back half of the house and smoke had begun to fill the room.

9:56 PM

Arthur noticed the orange glow just before the smell infiltrated his nose. His eyes widened when he made out the silhouette of a pitched roof.

The house? "Shit."

He was already moving as fast he could, the noise in his ears just a bland hum. He zigzagged toward the clearing, his head bobbing side to side weakly. His legs were liquid.

Finally, the woods cleared.

He pushed as hard as his body would allow, but it wasn't enough. He fell to his knees and then onto his chest, his face bouncing off the dry grass. His eyes tried to shut, but he forced them open. Simon stood on the porch, calculating how to get in and out without scorching himself. The man in gray peered down from the roof of the burning building, watching Simon. *How? Why was he up ...* Arthur's eyes shut and reopened. The man was near the edge now, jumping up and down on all fours, loosening the planks of wood just above Simon's head. One rolled off and struck Simon on the shoulder. He managed to jump back just before the next fell. It landed in front of him.

"Simon!" Arthur managed to yell.

Simon turned and found Arthur through squinted eyes, Arthur's waving hand catching his attention.

"I got them!" Simon yelled back. "They're in there. I can get to them."

It was useless. Arthur could not hear a thing.

Codi burst through the tree line. "Simon, get the hell away from there!"

The man in gray was prying loose boards from all over the roof, flinging them up in the air. They rained down.

"I found the box," Simon yelled to her, dipping his head and covering it with his arms. He leaned into the doorway, testing himself.

The books. He's after the books, Arthur thought. "Fuck the books!" he croaked, but it was too low for either of them to hear. He yelped in agony as the pain surged through his brain, and he curled into a fetal position. He slipped out of consciousness again as Codi skirted closer to Simon.

"Simon, leave them! There's someone on the roof!"

That snapped Simon's attention away from the box. He hopped down from the broken porch and aimed the gun up above him.

"He's right there!"

"Where?"

"To the left!"

The man in gray stood still near the peak of the roof. Flames began poking through the top now.

"I don't see him."

"You don't see him!" Codi shrieked. "He's right in front of you!"

"For fuck's sake, Codi, there's no one up there!"

The gray man disappeared behind the house.

In his strange silence, a lullaby began to play in Arthur's ears. A white glow washed away reality. When the singing began, it was his mother's voice, softly reciting *Sweet Child O' Mine*.

"Mom, how do you know this?"

"I hear you sing it to May," she said. "I like hearing you sing a happy song to her."

"I didn't want to sing a sad song. Why do we sing such sad songs to our children?"

"Because sadness is tiring."

"You're right."

The glow roiled.

"Bring May home," she said.

"I want to. I want to bring them all home."

"You can't."

"I can. I am."

"No, you can't."

He could hear Simon and Codi crowing somewhere around him, their voices muted and almost unrecognizable. If he had not known they were there, he would have disregarded the sounds as nothing at all.

"May is all that matters," she said. "Bring May home." Her voice shrank. Consciousness returned, as did pain.

"Bring her home," he repeated.

His eyes were glued shut, like he had slept for hours. When he wrenched them open, everyone was in the same place. Codi gestured madly to Simon. Simon stubbornly refused to back down.

Arthur peered over at Simon. "Bring her home," he repeated again in his stupor.

His ears were ready to explode, and he cried out. With each movement, something scratched at the inside of his ear canal like tiny jigsaws cutting toward his brain. He reached up, pinched his nose shut, and blew as hard as he could. A whistling whipped through his head and a thunderous crack relieved the pressure. A warm sensation took over as more blood dribbled from his right ear, followed by puss and clear fluid. The hearing in his left ear returned immediately and everything was strikingly loud, forcing him to cover his ears at first. "Simon!" he yelled out, struggling to his feet. "Simon get the fuck away from the house! Let it burn."

A loud bang rattled the ground around them, followed swiftly by screaming.

"The books are in there!" Simon shouted back, clearly tired of saying it to both Arthur and Codi, the latter of whom was now just behind Arthur.

"Fuck the books," Arthur yelled, stumbling toward Simon. "It's the goddamn house. Let it burn.

Let it destroy it all."

Codi climbed onto the sorry excuse for a porch and grabbed Simon by the arm, pulling him down with her. A wild flame peered from the doorway, reaching out for the two of them.

A loud whooping jolted the three of them backwards. Simon instinctively turned his head. The sound continued for a few seconds and then dissipated into the night.

"Did we kill it?" Codi asked. No one answered.

Simon holstered his gun, and the three of them stared at the cabin, three quarters of it now engulfed in flame. It would not be long until the entire structure would succumb.

"What are you going to do?" Simon asked.

"I don't know," Arthur said after some time. "But fuck this place. It wasn't going to let us get the books from the very beginning. Let's go home."

Simon pulled away and Codi and Arthur watched him. He bent over and picked up the one notebook that lay in the dirt and handed it to Arthur. "Bullshit."

As Arthur took it from Simon's hands, there was a moan from somewhere deep in the woods. Codi looked up to the roof, checking for any sign of the gray man. Arthur noticed and put his hand on her back, urging her to walk. "Ignore it. All of it."

She looked at him with tears in her eyes. "I'm sorry."

"Me too," he said.

Another moan echoed pathetically through the

woods.

10:00 PM

John Braun stared east down Route 223 from his place in front of the five and dime. He'd questioned whether the first moan was more than just his imagination, but the second one confirmed it. He stared at Arthur's business card in his hand, smiled, and slipped it back into his pocket.

"Good job, my friend."

Delilah shuffled to her feet as he began walking west.

11.

They expected to hear sirens, but the sounds never came. Not while they were there. But Simon drove quickly.

The first half of the ride was quiet as the three of them processed what had happened. Codi sat in the back with Arthur, pressing a towel to his ear and catching anything that leaked out as he rested his head against the door. He was still deaf in his right ear.

Simon leaned his elbow on the center armrest and recoiled at the pain. He rubbed it, and that was when he felt the swelling, a knot the size of a golf ball.

"You okay?" Arthur asked from the back seat.

"Yeah."

"Simon, I'm sorry, man."

"For what?"

"Dragging you into this. I should've known this wouldn't go down smoothly. And that you wouldn't bail if it didn't." Arthur held his bleeding knuckles against the bottom of his shirt, trying to avoid staining the seats.

Simon laughed. "The only thing I was worried about on the drive here was whether or not you were losing your goddamned mind." He elevated his arm by wrapping it around the back of the passenger seat. "And now I'm worried that I am." Both Arthur and Codi saw the lump and discoloration on his elbow. "A half hour can change a lot of shit. I've got some reevaluating to do."

"Thank you," said Arthur. "You're a good person. And I'm still sorry I dragged you into this." He looked over at Codi. "And thank you for ignoring me and doing what you wanted anyway." He laughed and put his hand on her knee. "You've helped me so much."

Codi cleared her throat. "I know you won't want to hear it, but we should probably get you to the hospital."

He smiled. "Tomorrow. I'll go in the morning. I just want to go home."

"That makes two of us," said Simon. "But she's right."

"The pain is gone. I'm fine. It can wait. You might need to get that softball looked at, though."

"I'll ice it." He bent it back and forth before putting his arm in his lap.

Arthur looked at the book on the floor between his feet. Ninety-five percent of him did not want to know what it contained. Not only because he was emotionally and physically drained, but because he knew the other books were just as important. And he would never see them again.

"Simon, can I smoke in your car?"

"Not usually, no. But knock yourself out."

He reached for his pack but changed his mind. Instead, he watched the black trees whizz by, closing his eyes every once in a while. He saw May's face each time. Just as he dozed, he felt his phone vibrate in his pocket. He removed it and read the text message on the screen.

It was from Sarah.

"I can't tell you how sorry I am for the way I've been. I love you, and I miss you. Please call me tomorrow."

He frowned.

"Everything okay?" asked Codi.

He looked her in the eyes, and then closed his, dropping his head back to the window. She dropped her own head onto the headrest in the center of the backseat. To her right, on the empty cushion, was her sneaker from the day before.

10:54 PM

"I can get myself in," Arthur said, leaning up against Simon's truck. "Codi, get home to Cara. You guys have done enough." He looked back to Simon, his elbow at an awkward angle, unable to straighten out. "Go home and rest. I'll tattoo you whenever you want."

"Sorry you didn't get what you wanted," he said.

Arthur held up the notebook. "Maybe it'll work out."

"Come on," he said, guiding Arthur by the arm. Codi wrapped Arthur's other arm around her shoulder, and they helped him along the path to the front of the house. He pushed the door open and walked inside.

"You guys want a water or something before you go?" he asked, turning to them. "I have coffee. I'll throw it into a paper cup so you can take it with you." He slicked his hair out of his face. Bits of leaf tumbled out.

"I'm cool," said Simon. "I'm only a few blocks away." His phone rang.

"Do you want to come home with me?" Codi asked. "I have the room, if you don't want to be alone," she said.

"Melinda? What's up?" Simon said into his phone, walking away from the both of them.

"No, I'll be fine," Arthur said, smiling. "Will *you* be okay by yourself? That was some serious shit."

"I've got the folks," she said. "Built-in therapists."

Arthur laughed. "I wish I could call my mom." Oddly, he felt as though her voice was fresh in his mind. He liked that.

"Wait, what?" said Simon. "No, I haven't heard from him. What are you talking about? Why would he call me at eleven o'clock at night? Did you call Chris's parents to see if he went there?" He paused for a response. "Melinda, how the hell does an eleven-year-old boy just disappear!"

Arthur stared emptily at Simon. From inside the house, a baby began to cry.

THANK YOU

A sincere thank you for reading this book. The feeling is indescribable when I am able to share my creations with another person. It's hard to resist succumbing to a passion, never mind trying to make a living doing it. It is because of readers like you that I am able to make an attempt. For that, I will be forever grateful, and I will consistently put out the best material I possibly can.

If you have some extra time, be sure to rate **The Committed** anywhere you see it, and check out www.JustinMermelstein.com to sign up for my mailing list and for information on future work.

Justin Mermelstein
New Jersey, 2015

www.ingramcontent.com/pod-product-compliance
Lightning Source LLC
Chambersburg PA
CBHW021227130626
46554CB00004B/1394

* 9 7 8 0 9 8 8 6 6 8 7 4 4 *